THE WINDEBY PUZZLE

ALSO BY LOIS LOWRY

THE
WINDEBY
PUZZLE

HISTORY AND STORY

LOIS LOWRY

CLARION BOOKS

An Imprint of HarperCollins*Publishers*

For my German family:
Margret, Jürgen, Nadine, and Sinuhe

CONTENTS

THE WINDEBY PUZZLE

PART ONE

HISTORY

"Hold it! Stop the engine!"
The heavy machinery fell silent. The operator peered
down from the cab. "Why? What's wrong?"
"Look! We pulled up a leg!"
"Holy—" The workers fell silent. They stared at the
thing dangling from the metal digging claw.
"Think it's from a stag?" one asked, finally.
But they all knew it wasn't an animal's leg. It was
human.

It was May 1952, on an estate called Windeby in
northern Germany. Workmen using modern cutting equipment were removing peat from a small

bog the day that one of them saw what he thought at first was a large animal bone. It wasn't. It was a human lower leg, and they quickly discovered that their machinery had also brought up a foot and a hand. Thinking they had unearthed a crime scene, they turned off their equipment and summoned the police.

A museum curator and his assistants also rushed to the scene. After an examination of what had been found almost five feet below the surface of the bog, they explained to the police that this was not an unsolved murder—at least, not in the usual sense. These body parts, scientists eventually determined, were around two thousand years old, from the first century AD, the time now known as the Iron Age. The workmen had uncovered what was known as a "bog body," which means just that: a body found buried in a peat bog. Hundreds of them have been discovered over the last two centuries. The oldest is a Danish woman known to anthropologists as Koelbjerg Woman, who died around 8000 BC.

Peat is a curious substance. It is created in wetlands where vegetation—plants, grasses, moss—never fully decays because of a high acid content. This organic semi-decayed material, peat, builds up over centuries to become a thick, mucky, and waterlogged swamp, or bog. Harvested, compressed, and dried, peat has been used as fuel for countless years; it still is, in some places. In earlier days, chunks of peat were dug by hand, using spades, then dried and piled beside primitive farmhouses. More recently, sophisticated mechanical equipment does the same job of cutting and compressing the substance. Today you can find peat moss, a substance harvested from peat, for sale in garden centers along with fertilizer and compost; adding it to your garden will help the soil retain moisture.

At night, in a peat bog, gases produced by the bog materials ignite when they encounter oxygen, creating flickering lights that scientists call bio-luminescence. Not surprisingly, folklore and ghost stories sometimes portray the phenomena as sinister spirits, beckoning to travelers. No question, peat bogs are spooky, sometimes dangerous places. And, as the German peat-cutters discovered in 1952, they contain secrets.

The high acid content that permeates a peat bog, combined with the climate in northern Europe, creates an odd kind of refrigerated morgue. Bodies placed in a bog decompose very, very slowly. Although the thick skull remains intact, smaller bones eventually disintegrate while at the same time, the bog chemicals preserve the skin, hair, and nails. Found centuries later, some of the dead are said to resemble deflated rubber dolls. There are expressions on their faces, and the men have stubble on their chins. Some have trimmed fingernails, and hair carefully braided and arranged.

Most of the bog bodies, sadly, had died violent deaths. Their remains tell us that. There is evidence of horrific injuries: bashed skulls, nooses around their necks, stab wounds. We don't know why. Were these people criminals, singled out for execution? Or perhaps they may have been sacrificial victims, chosen to assuage the gods, to ensure a better harvest? In the first century AD, Christianity had not yet made its way to northern Europe. But the people of that era had pagan gods—Wotan, Donar, and Nerthus, the earth mother, among others—whom they tried to please with rites and rituals. Human sacrifice was occasionally one of those.

"Young," the anthropologists announced, after studying the body that had been carefully removed from the Windeby bog in 1952. That was rare. Most of the bog bodies found until then had been adults.

Adolescent female, they decided. A young girl, maybe thirteen. Small in stature, they could tell, though much of her lower body had been destroyed by the weight of the peat and the machinery of the peat-cutters.

She wore no clothes except a small animal hide around her neck and shoulders. And she had been blindfolded. A strip of cloth, intricately woven to create a pattern of brown, yellow, and red, encircled her head and covered her eyes.

She had no wounds, no indications of violence. The expression on her face was serene. Her hair, what remained, was blond. But mysteriously, the left side of her head had been shaved.

The laboratories and museums that contain and study the bog bodies have given them names based on the places where they had been found. Lindow

Man and Worsley Man were discovered in England. Tollund Man, Grauballe Man, and Elling Woman, in Denmark. In Ireland: Gallagh Man and Clonycavan Man. North Germany had uncovered Damendorf Man in 1900. And now, this slight, golden-haired teenager. They called her Windeby Girl.

Each of us has a story. I do, you do, my mailman does; so does the frail elderly neighbor, the woman who waits on me at the supermarket, and the boy who just rode past me on a bicycle.

Our stories each have a beginning, middle, and— eventually—an ending. We have adventures along the way. We have moments of anger and despair, times we are bored and distracted, spells of quiet contentment, and other times when we are overwhelmed by joy.

We live out our stories in various locations. Some of us, perhaps, end where we start, without ever having explored other realms. Others find it hard to stay put.

Me? I was born on a tropical island. I moved, later, to a big city, then to a small town, then to another city in a different country, then to another, and another, and another. I had siblings. Along the way, I was educated. Eventually I married and had four children. I lived in different kinds of houses: big ones, small ones, old ones, new ones. I had dogs and cats, several horses along the way, and once (briefly) a pet raccoon. A bicycle and another bicycle . . . and cars, and more cars, and more. I went back again for more education. I chose a career. My children grew up. One died. I loved, and I was loved. I grew old.

Those facts are not particularly interesting. But when I embellish them with the details that surround each fact—and what those details meant, how important they were—then the story is filled out, and raises questions, and takes on meaning, and the story gradually becomes *me*.

Part of the *me* is a storyteller. I like to pry open doors, and peer into corners, and figure out all the *why*s that make people who they are.

When I read for the first time about the Windeby Girl, I was consumed with curiosity. Who was this small-in-stature, middle school–age blond person?

She seemed so like my own young self. I thought back to seventh grade, when in gym class we girls were asked to line up by height. I trudged to the end of the line, knowing that as always I was the shortest, the smallest of my classmates. Sure, there were some who were only slightly taller; we shorties giggled, poked at each other, and peered down the line, which grew gradually until at the other end stood the girls I envied, the ones who were already taller and more mature. I would grow, of course, and by the time I was, oh, fifteen or so, I was full-size and more self-confident.

But the Windeby Girl never had that chance. Why not? What had happened to her?

I began to think about jigsaw puzzles, how one examines each piece, looking for clues of shape and color, until things fit together and the entire picture emerges. I wanted to solve the puzzle of this young girl, to learn her story.

Some of that story had been already been determined by science. Radiocarbon dating is a chemical analysis used to identify the age of organic materials based on their content of the radioisotope carbon-14.

The process had been developed in 1946 (Willard Libby won the Nobel Prize in Chemistry for his contributions to it) and so was newly available when the Windeby Girl was found six years later. It had revealed that she had lived in the first century AD: the Iron Age, a time when people had begun to fashion swords, saws, scythes, hammers, and farming tools from iron. The Germanic tribes of that period left no writings, no records. So we have to use other sources to find the clues, to begin to understand their lives. And after those sources give out, we can only guess.

I started by exploring what facts I could find. Archaeologists have excavated dwellings and villages that existed in that century, and I studied the photographs and drawings, creating in my mind the kind of daily life that . . . *No, wait,* I told myself. *Before you try to create the life she had lived . . .*

She needed a name. I chose one from the long lists of old Germanic female names.

I called her Estrild.

Then, named, she became real to me. She entered a world that I would create: a world of family, friends, animals, and a daily life that, like every life in every century, would be filled with hardships and delights, struggles and successes. As I envisioned her surroundings, I placed her there, in my mind. I could see her standing beside a primitive dwelling with a thatched roof, with forest behind the village, cultivated farmland nearby, and of course the dank bog that would eventually be her resting place. She looked at me with blue eyes and raised one hand to smooth back her long blond hair.

I began to write her story. *The spring wind was cold*, I wrote. *Estrild wrapped her shawl around her and fastened it with the curved bone clasp she had created from the skeleton of a bird . . .*

I had read, actually, of such a clasp, found with another one of the bog bodies, though not the Windeby Girl.

But I paused before I could continue, before I could create a narrative that would invite readers to share Estrild's story. I paused because I found myself terribly sad. Despite what adventures I might give to her, what friends, what girlish laughter I might describe— still, I knew the story would end in tragedy. I glanced over at the book on the table beside me; it was open to the page with her photograph. The small, delicate nose. The lips, slightly parted, as if she were about to speak. The seashell-like curvature of her ear.

No matter what details and activities I could create to give her an imagined life, it would still end when she was thirteen years old, dead in a bog, with a woven blindfold over her eyes. Why?

The scientists who first examined her had come up with two theories, two possible explanations. They were able to do so, in part, because a Roman historian named Tacitus had written, late in the first century AD, an account of the Germanic tribes in northern Europe, the location where the Windeby Girl had been found.

He described the people of the region as being blue eyed, very often with red hair (though my Estrild was blond), and large of stature—*huge frames*, he wrote. Yet she was so small. Perhaps she stood out, being petite? Did that make her special in some way? (But I was getting ahead of myself, imagining her story once again.)

They fought each other, these Germanic tribes,

and Tacitus told us that they had a ritual of song before battle. He said they kindled their courage by singing, and that their songs were harsh and roaring, that they "put their shields before their mouths in order to make the voice swell fuller and deeper as it echoes back." It made me think of New Zealand's Maori, of their hakas. I'd gone to YouTube again and again to watch those fierce, stylized rituals; now, reading Tacitus, I wondered if my fictitious girl, my Estrild, had trembled, listening to the men and boys of her tribe practicing their war chants that were called, Tacitus tells us, *barritas*. Somehow, I decided, I would add that to her story.

He described, also, the role of women in the tribal communities. This part captured my interest. Marriage rituals required that the men present a dowry, gifts that the bride's parents looked over and approved: oxen, horses, shields, and spears. Women were highly respected, and the wife was reminded, according to Tacitus, that she was to "share a man's toils and dangers, that in peace and war alike she is to be his partner in all his sufferings and achievements."

Being partner in her husband's toils and dangers did not mean, though, that she accompanied him in warfare. How could she? The wives of the Germanic tribes were busy from dawn to dusk. She planted the crops, prepared the food, and wove the cloth from which she made the family's clothing, and she did it all while keeping an eye on her many children while frequently pregnant with the next. Tacitus recounted quite clearly that a wife was expected to bear children—and not to restrict their number; to do so was a criminal act—to breastfeed them, and above all else, to be faithful. Adultery brought harsh and unpardonable punishment, which included the shaving of the woman's hair.

It was the Roman historian's mention of the shaved head that led scholars to guess a possible reason for the death of the young Windeby girl. Perhaps, they suggested, she had had an illicit love affair with a married man. They theorized that she would have been shorn of half her hair, publicly humiliated, taunted, stripped naked, blindfolded, and drowned in the nearby bog.

A frightening and dramatic story that made me cringe. But I also found it hard to believe. I looked again at the photograph of the doomed girl and to me there seemed no hint of sophistication or worldliness. Estrild was a child on the threshold of adolescence. If she had any experience with girlish romance, it would have been no more than shy, awkward flirtations. Perhaps, watching the teenage boys rehearse for battles still in the future, stomping and singing their harsh chants, she secretly thought one more handsome than another.

So the story I was creating for my Windeby girl would not find her getting caught in the forest with someone's husband. It didn't ring true to me.

The second explanation, horrific though it was, made slightly more sense.

The Germanic tribes worshipped many deities, Tacitus says. They appeased some of the gods with offerings of "beasts" (probably cattle, goats, or lambs), and they also, on some occasions, practiced human sacrifice. It was from that note of Tacitus that the scientists studying the Windeby Girl created another theory: that the young virgin might, in fact, have been sacrificed, perhaps after a hard winter and poor crops, in an attempt to cajole the gods into a better harvest next season.

Tacitus even describes their methods of selection of the sacrificial victim, the way they drew lots using small wood strips from a fruit tree, peeled of bark, marked with mysterious symbols, and cast onto a white cloth for the priests, who were called druids, to decipher.

Though I found it more plausible than the punishment-for-adultery explanation, it was still a grim and terrible ending for the petite blond youngster I had already begun to care about. Was there any other story possible? Tacitus had also said in passing: "Those who disgrace their bodies are drowned in miry swamps." That's an intriguing, mysterious reference, but it's not entirely clear what he meant by it. I decided to think about that one.

But I wouldn't decide on an ending right away. I'd simply imagine a young girl opening a door early on a spring morning. That would start her story. And maybe, with luck, with imagination, it would take me someplace surprising.

PART TWO

ESTRILD'S
STORY

THE WARRIOR'S KNOT

Cool wind.

Day start. One bird a-twitter. Warblers newly back now, settling in, after winter in a warmer place.

Planting time soon. Then the birds would be everywhere: noisy, pecking for the seeds, for the insects. Eggs in the nests: speckled eggs they were, the warblers' nests in the high grasses.

Dark, still. But the land was alive: waking, whistling with breeze through the grasses and murmuring with creatures emerging from sleep. The ox in his nearby pen snorted and shifted his weight. An owl, high up, aware of rabbits scampering back to their burrows, gave a breathy, repetitive hoot.

Estrild, standing just outside the doorway, shivered, wrapped her shawl around her, and fastened it with a peeled thorn. When she had time— there was a laugh! Who ever had time? there were always the chores—but when she could, on a stormy day perhaps, she would try to smooth and polish the small bony skeleton of a bird she had hidden away; she had a plan to make it into a clasp to hold her shawl edges tight.

A woman in the village had such a clasp. Estrild had noticed it during the autumn ceremonies. The druids intoned their spells, the men thumped their spears into the ground, chanting, and the women watched from the edge, jiggling the babies and murmuring soothing sounds to quiet the hungry whimpers. Through it all, from her place standing on the edge, Estrild had noticed the tall red-haired woman, had studied the curved brooch, measuring how a sharpened piece of bone thrust through the woven cloth—in and then out—held the fringed edges of fabric together and made a sort of decoration.

Not that she wanted decoration. But she liked the idea of the little skeleton, the remains of a creature taking on a new role, reminding one that it had existed. Usually dead things—even people!—crumbled and rotted away and were forgotten.

For now, though, for holding the borders of her shawl tight, the jagged thorn would do. Estrild adjusted the fastening securely. She rubbed her hands together to warm them, moved away from the dooryard, and felt her way along the darkened path that divided dwellings one from another. She headed toward the edge of the small village.

"Estrild?" The voice came, a hoarse whisper, from the entranceway of the shadowed storage shed behind the iron-forger's hut. The hut was a separate structure, apart from the village dwellings, alone in its patch of land. The forger used fire. All dwellings had a fire for warmth and cooking, but the iron-forger, especially, kept his ablaze and flaring; he made sparks, hammering at pieces of iron, shaping tools and spears and shields. His forge was set apart, for safety. They all feared fire. Their dwellings were built of twigs and sticks and thatch; whole villages had been destroyed in the past by flames. So the forger's hut was separate, and the flaming bits that were sometimes thrown loose landed in dirt and died there.

Hearing the husky voice, the girl peered over through the shadows and laughed. "Varick!" she said. "Good! You remembered. No need to hide. Everyone is asleep still. Come on out."

A thin boy with long unkempt hair emerged from the shed. He was older than Estrild, but less healthy. He was hunched over, and his bones showed, elbows knobby, and his ribs laddering his chest behind a ragged open vest. He nodded a greeting and followed her along the wide dirt lane. He walked awkwardly. His back was crooked, and it made his gait uneven; he lurched. Sometimes she had seen him lean on a stick. But this morning he had left his stick behind because with both hands he carried something that glistened in the dim predawn.

"You still look like a boy," he said to her suddenly.

She peered through the darkness to look at him. "I know that," she told him.

"Not too long, though, and you'll be womanly."

"I know *that*, too."

"Just thinking that now's the time you can do this."

"Yes. I've been planning it for a long time, been yearning for it, but when I was younger I was too scared, and too small. If I don't do it now, though, it will be too late." She turned off the lane into a narrow path bordered by tall grass. "Come this way," she said, and waited to be certain he was following. "I have a place in mind. Near the place where you showed me the bird skeleton once—remember?"

"You still have it?" he asked.

She nodded. "Yes." She had become friends with the odd, solitary boy when she was young. She had often observed him doing his chores at the forge or greeted him as they both waited in line for water from the village well. One afternoon, on a meadow path, she had come across him hunched over the remains of a dead bird—something most people would kick aside. Varick, though, had held it cupped in his dirty hand and, when she stopped to look, he explained the parts to her: how the bones worked, how complicated even the smallest creature was. He studied such things, he had told her. Even bugs and worms. It was his secret, he had said.

And so, eventually, she had shared her own secret with the boy: the longing that consumed her, the thing that had brought her here this dawn.

"How old are *you*?" she asked, as they went forward into the meadow. Estrild was familiar with such details about most of her friends in the village. But this friendship was private, unshared. And she knew nothing of the boy's history.

"Not sure."

"Why don't you know?"

"My mother died when I was born. So nobody kept watch of my age."

"Who fed you?"

"My father gave me to a neighbor to tend. He

paid her coins so she'd feed me. But after he was gone there were no more coins, so she put me out."

"Where did your father go?"

"He died in battle. My father was a warrior." Though the shadows, she could see Varick hold himself straighter, signaling his pride. It was worthy of pride, to have a warrior in the family, though to lose a warrior in battle was too frequent a thing. Estrild was still washed with grief when she remembered her mother's younger brother, Erhard, her beloved uncle, killed by a spear thrust just last year, in a skirmish over rulership of nearby land.

They said, afterward, that Erhard had led a charge across a field, had called his battle cry in a loud and fearless voice. In the midst of it one of his fellow warriors had been struck by an arrow. Erhard had paused to give him aid, had crouched in a moment of kindness to help his friend, and was lost when an enemy warrior on horseback galloped past with his spear.

Estrild remembered how Erhard's blue eyes had crinkled with amusement as he had tickled and teased her just days before that battle, how the villagers had cheered him and his fellow warriors as they marched off to warfare with their spears thumping the ground in rhythm. And she could still see, in her memory, her uncle's blood-smeared face and how his death-stopped eyes had stared unseeing at the sky as they carried him, splayed atop his shield, up the path a week later.

The tribes, so many of them scattered across these hillsides, had vied throughout history. The bards sang of warfare centuries past; in those sung tales, the warriors of the earlier times were often aided by gods who came to earth and took sides. Now the deities remained distant, though the druids still intoned prayers before battles, asking for their help.

"What did you do after your father died?" she asked Varick.

The boy shrugged. "Grabbed what I could, here and there."

Her own life, Estrild thought, was hard, with all the chores and the constant help her mother needed with so many little ones. But Varick's had been so much harder. He'd worked just to survive, and it seemed that he'd barely made it. No wonder he was so thin. His breath came hard as he limped beside her.

"I can carry that," she told him, and reached over to try to lighten his burden.

"You take this one," he said, and handed her one of the gleaming objects. "Other one's for me, to show you how."

He handed her a large circular shield. In the dim light she ran her fingers over the hammered pattern.

"It's not done yet," Varick explained. "He's still working on it."

"Who will it go to?"

"One of the new warriors. He'll have it at the ceremony."

The ceremony. That was the time she was waiting for, working toward. And it would be soon.

"We have time, don't we, before the ceremony? For you to teach me? How long do you think it will take?"

Varick sighed, and she fell silent. He was willing to teach her, but she knew he thought her plan foolish. More than foolish: dangerous. And perhaps it was. But she felt stirred to try. Maybe it was a need for vengeance, for Erhard, the uncle she had loved— and, now that she knew of him, for Varick's father, who had fallen in battle and left an orphaned son. Women should not let such losses go unanswered.

But more than that, her longing had begun with observing her mother. Estrild had watched her mother day after day with a feeling that grew stronger each year: the feeling that life should hold more for a woman. She could remember a time, perhaps six or seven summers before, when her mother had been strong, had run laughing with her in the meadow where their horse was pastured, had lifted her to the horse's back and sprung easily up behind her, had grabbed the thick mane, and galloped with her as the wind caught their hair and their voices.

But laughter had long ago left their dwelling. Her mother, once so lively, was stooped, now, the skin on her face hardened into lines, and her fingers were gnarled at the joints; a potion made from willow bark eased the pain of them, but it came back threefold each time the weather turned damp. The same had happened, was happening still, to the other village wives and mothers. At the ceremonies and festivals it was always the boys and men who were cheered and celebrated. Never the women. Watching them, Estrild had begun to feel a passion to become more than just another wife, one more woman made gaunt from chores and childbearing, old before her time. Women deserved more.

"Here. This is the place," she said, pausing to look around. They had reached a small clearing.

"I have to get these back before the sun's up. He'll be looking for them."

"I know. So let's start," Estrild said. She slipped one hand into the handle on the back and raised the shield in front of her. "Like this?" she asked the boy.

He lifted his own in the same fashion and spoke around it.

"Yes. Like that."

"Is that one yours?" She reached forward, touched it, and felt the raised decorative symbols.

"It's beautiful. Did you get it in a ceremony? I don't remember seeing you called forward, but there are always a lot of new warriors and it's so noisy."

The boy gave a rueful laugh and lowered the shield. "*Me*? They'd never choose me a warrior. No, the forger's making this for Ralf. Ralf doesn't know yet, though. Don't say anything."

Estrild shrugged. "I won't. I never talk to him anyway." She knew Ralf only slightly. He had been rude to her once, when she was at the well; he had jostled her aside, pushing himself forward, announcing loudly that he was thirsty. But the boys his age were all of them rude, self-important and noisy. Ralf was a typical future warrior, like his friends, though a worse braggart than most. His ceremony would be full of boasting and shouting. And of course Varick, her knobby-kneed orphan friend, was different; she shouldn't even have asked about the shield and embarrassed him.

"Come over here," she told him, and moved to the edge of the clearing. "Let's do it here. No one can hear us."

She stopped, stood still, and planted her feet apart, with her knees bent slightly. The boy lowered his own shield and watched her. "Am I holding this properly?" she asked.

"Higher," he told her, and she adjusted so the shield hid her face.

Estrild had assumed the position easily; even though she was not as large or as strong as boys her age, she was lithe and agile. But when Varick responded by assuming the same stance—feet wide apart, knees bent, shield up—he was more awkward. She winced, watching him. He was so sickly; his walk was slowed by his limp, and he coughed as often as he spoke. Living as he did, curled into a corner of the blacksmith's storage shed at night, foraging for scraps to eat, wasn't healthy for him. She was fond of the boy and had sometimes wished that she could take him to her own dwelling, where at least there was some warmth in winter, and food. But her mother, who was once again with child—the eleventh, though several born during hard winters had not survived—would never allow that. The dwelling was crowded and noisy, with nothing to offer an ailing boy, even one like Varick who had a quick smile and generous heart.

So Ralf, with a prosperous and arrogant father, would have this finely decorated shield. And he would never know that a girl had been one of the first to touch it. Maybe, she thought wryly, she would tell him one day, when they were on a battlefield together.

"Now do this." Varick stamped one foot, then the other. His body swayed.

Estrild imitated him.

He began making harsh, guttural sounds. She had heard her brothers do this at times, when they were drinking. They did the warrior chant then, making a joke of it, though often it led to shoving and slapping until their mother shouted at the boys to take their foolish warfare outside—wasn't it enough that the little ones scuffled and bickered till her head ached?

Alard and Carolus, both of them warriors now, would be off next time there was a battle to be fought. Someday, perhaps soon, they would marry; they were working hard already, preparing the dowries they would present for the brides' parents to approve before a wedding could take place. Then her brothers would be gone, to their own dwellings, to their own brood of babies. But for now they took up space, ate a lot, and with their father drank the fermented apple liquid that made them quarrelsome and loud.

She stamped her feet again and tried to lower her voice and imitate the sounds Varick made. "Pull your shield close!" he called, interrupting his own performance, and demonstrated with his own.

She did, and made the harsh cries again, but now they fell against the hammered iron of the shield and echoed and grew loud. It startled her. She peered out at Varick and he laughed.

"Yes!" he said. "It makes it even more fierce!" He showed her, chanting first into the air, then into the shield, so that the volume was magnified. Estrild remembered and pictured, in her mind, the long row of warriors and the terrifying sound they could make; she had watched and heard them during the ceremonies each year.

She grunted and woofed into her shield. Varick did the same. Then they laughed at each other and did it again, trying to form a kind of chorus. Their feet—hers in laced foot-coverings of stretched hide, the boy's bare on the cold earth—drummed the ground while they barked and shouted the sounds into the shields.

Gradually they found a rhythm to it. They moved, copying each other. "*Barritas*," Varick said to her; she knew the word, which described the chant. They started: grunting first in unison, then back and forth, their sounds a kind of question and answer. Then they shifted their shields, changing the reverberation— soft, then loud; silence, then a yelp and roar. It— *barritas*—was the sound of true warriors: the sound that drove a spike of fear into their enemies.

She fell silent, breathless, then glanced up, suddenly. A thin strip of amber light had appeared, washing the edge of the tree-lined hills beyond the village. Time was short. "We must go," she told the boy. "We don't want anyone wondering where we are.

"Tomorrow?" she asked him as they headed from

the clearing to the meadow path. "Maybe earlier, so we have more time?"

Varick nodded. He reached for her shield as they approached the small shed behind the iron-forger's hut. "When you're alone," he said, "practice making the sounds to yourself."

"I will. But, Varick—the knot? When will you teach me the knot?"

"Soon."

"I've tried, by myself. But I can't get it right. If you'd just show me—"

"Soon," he repeated. "There's time, still."

"But—"

"I must hurry," he said. "Look, he's started the fire. That's my job, usually." Hastily, stealthily, he deposited the two shields in the storage shed near the mound of straw where he slept each night.

"Will he be angry that you were gone?" Estrild whispered.

"Yes. But if he asks, I'll tell him I went out to piss."

Estrild stood watching as Varick pulled his vest around him and headed toward the swept-earth area where she could see the iron-forger using bellows to enliven his morning fire. Sparks drifted upward as the fire began to breathe. She moved away, toward the path that would lead to her own dwelling, where she knew her mother would be awake now and expecting Estrild to help with the toddlers and the huge pot of morning gruel. Briefly she looked back. She wished she could call to Varick, to thank him. But he was already at the forge; she could see his crooked silhouette against the light made by the invigorated fire. So she bit her tongue, turned away, and ran one hand through her long tangle of blond hair. She had wanted to ask him about the next morning, to remind him again that in addition to the warrior stance and chant, she must begin to learn about the knot. It was the knot that would truly change her from a useless girl into a warrior. The first woman warrior.

The village was small. It nestled against a hillside, with the crop fields spreading across the flatter land below. The large smelting furnace, the place where iron was released from the rocks where it was found, stood at a distance, with the iron-forger's hut and shed nearby. At the other end of the main path was the longhouse where the druids lived and where they taught the boys chosen as their successors. Between, spread across the base of the hill and joined by paths, lay the dwellings, smoke wafting from each chimney and curling across the thatched roofs. In a central open space the various sheds and huts for goldsmithing, pottery-making, woodworking, leatherwork, were arranged in a sort of ring around the village well.

In these early daybreak moments, chickens pecked and scrabbled in the dooryards. Larger creatures—goats, sheep, an occasional horse or cow or ox—were encircled by fences made of tree branches. They shifted and stirred as they woke and waited for their morning toss of hay. In the hives, bees woke and buzzed, emerging now from their winter silence. Below the dwellings, beyond the marsh with its high grasses, a large pond shimmered in the first light, the spring breeze rippling its surface.

Estrild hurried past the leather-maker's hut, where her father spent his long days, and the pottery shed with its large rounded kiln. She reached her family's home and slipped noiselessly through the entrance, glad to see that her absence had gone unnoticed; her mother's attention was on the large pot that she had lowered by its chain to the fire. The thick air inside the dwelling had changed with the coming of spring. Now the animals, accustomed to sleeping near their humans through the winter season, were out of doors, and the dwelling no longer smelled of them, their matted and bug-infested coats, their steamy droppings and breathy snorts. Now the smell was of the peaty fire, the smoke of which ascended to the chimney hole and curled around the dried meats hanging from the high poles that held the structure firm.

The little ones were noisy and cross, as Estrild had known they would be. They bickered and poked at each other, scuffling on the sleeping mats while her mother, ignoring them, stirred the thick mixture of barley gruel in the heavy pot. Estrild grabbed a small boy and held him wriggling against her.

"I'll wash Bruno," she told her mother, and carried the protesting boy to the door of the dwelling while his fists drummed against her shoulders. "You come too, Berta," she added, and the other toddler, a girl, grabbed at the hem of Estrild's skirt and followed, bare feet stumbling on the uneven earth floor. Outside, she stood them side by side and scrubbed at their faces and hands with a cloth dampened from the water pot that stood beside the entrance. Their upper lips were both crusted with snot. They always had colds. Estrild wiped the runny noses, smoothed their tangled hair, and let them play with twigs, twirling patterns into the stored water, until their hands were good and wet. Then she dried them both with the cloth that hung from a peg and turned them loose. They scurried back inside and she watched as her mother filled two more bowls for these youngest. It was noisy, now, in the dwelling; the other children, Hilda and Lotte, ten-year-old twin girls, were at the large table, eating and arguing. Estrild shook her head when her mother offered her a bowl. She tore off a piece of bread, dipped it in the clay pitcher that held milk, and made a breakfast of it.

"Where's Father?" she asked. "And the lads?"

Her mother shrugged, smoothed her apron around the mound of her belly, and sat down. "The boys went off to plow. It's soon time to plant the back field again."

They rotated the fields, fencing the animals in them some years, to fertilize and to let the soil rest from planting.

"And your father's helping to prepare the grove for the ceremony."

The ceremony. Of course. She and Varick had just spoken of it. It was spring now and would be time soon—next full moon—for the festival held in the sacred grove each year at the end of winter. It was the ritual that gave thanks for last fall's harvest, which had gotten them though the harshest season, and which would summon the gods, especially Nerthus, the earth mother, to grant them a plentiful and abundant season of crops to come. There would be prayers and rites, with the druids droning the names of the many gods, and the villagers murmuring in response. There would be the squeals and shrieks from sacrificial animals and the hush while the druids examined the steaming entrails for portents and omens. After that, the council would gather to consider disputes and mete punishments for crimes. Then there would be the manhood ceremonies, with the calling out of the names of those young boys deemed worthy of becoming warriors; they would come forward with their shields, chanting and growling their *barritas*, pretending it was new to them, though they'd been rehearsing their own warrior voices secretly throughout the winter.

Finally, there would be food and music and dancing, though the dancing would turn eventually to shoving and kicking, because there would be drink, too, and the men, the warriors, would brawl and shout and puke in their drunkenness. At least it would be a celebration and even the drunkenness would be of a happy sort, not like the winter three years ago, which Estrild remembered well. The crops had failed after heavy spring rains were followed by summer drought. That year her mother had given birth to an autumn child, a boy that lived only a short time and died unnamed, unnourished, scrawny and silent. That spring's festival had been grim, with long, imploring chants from the druids mingled with piercing squeals as the sacrificial blood spurted and seeped onto the stones, all of it a chorus against the low moan and wail of the women who recalled not only their dying children but also the wasted, skeletal elders who had not lasted through the cold time either. Estrild had stood to the side, hating the sounds, hungry, and resenting her own needs.

But this spring would be different.

"It will be joyful this year," she said to her mother, who nodded in agreement but murmured, "It's a hopeful time, but we must never expect things—"

"I do! I expect the fields to be full of crops and there will be just enough rain, and I expect everyone's babies will be born healthy, and I expect there will be weddings and feasts and . . . and . . ."

"Shhh. Don't make the gods angry with your talk. We'll work hard and take what comes."

Estrild sighed. "Do you never feel joyful, Mother?"

Her mother didn't reply. But after a moment she gestured to her weaving loom against the far wall.

"Look! I'll take it off the loom soon." She was pointing to the fabric she'd been working on for so many days. "It will be ready for you for the festival."

Estrild nodded. The fabric fell into folds of color, its dyed yarns—yellow, brown, red—crisscrossing themselves into the pattern her mother had created. It was unusual for her mother to have worked so hard, spent so much of her time, weaving this lengthy, colorful piece of cloth. Mostly she stood at the upright wooden loom each day, moving her hands in long-practiced rhythms, turning out practical, no-color fabrics from the spun wool: wrappings for the infant to come, bed coverings, pieces to be shaped and stitched into tunics for the men. But this was different. Over the winter the spun wool from their sheep had been soaked in dyes—madder root for the red, onionskin for yellow, and nut hulls to create the brown—then dried and sorted and arranged and fed carefully onto the loom to create this intricate design that her mother planned to drape upon Estrild, who was to display it proudly at the festival.

"Why don't you wear it, Mother?"

"Me? With my belly like this?" Her mother laughed. "No, this is for my eldest daughter. You will be the most beautiful girl there."

"I don't want to. I don't care about beautiful."

"Not yet. But you will. You'll soon be a woman. You will be looking for a husband, for a—"

Estrild interrupted her. "I'll go milk the goats," she said. She turned away.

Her mother would never understand. Neither did her friends, the other village girls her age. They wanted all that: the beauty, the sidelong looks of admiration from young warriors. But Estrild's passion was someplace else. She thirsted for what the boys had: the strength. The *power*.

Making her way to the goat pen, she stayed silent. But in her mind she was rehearsing again the low chants, the grunts and muffled roars of the warrior cries echoing in the hollow of the shield. *Barritas*.

Estrild glanced up as she milked and could see her older brothers in the field struggling with the plow and the massive, silent ox. The ox was old now; he had been part of her parents' marriage dowry; her mother said that her father had brought it to her proudly with a garland of flowers wreathed upon its neck. Now its ribs showed and its hide was patchy and scarred.

She watched as Carolus leaned down and wrested a large rock from the earth before the plow could move ahead. He lifted it, carried it aside, and dropped it at the field's edge. She could see that his long hair was sweaty and damp. The sun was strong now and made the boys' shoulders glisten. The two of them, Carolus and Alred, were hard workers—handsome, too; the young women of marriage age were flirtatious with them, and the boys teased them back. Estrild, watching them, hoped that warfare wouldn't cut their lives short as it had her uncle's.

She wondered sadly what would become of her friend Varick. He would reach marrying age soon. But he would have no way to raise dowry gifts for a girl, and no girl would want him anyway, with his twisted back and skinny chest. He'd never be able to plow a field or even to take over the ironwork.

The iron-forger worked throughout the daylight hours in the fire heat; his face was always smudged from the smoke, and his thick arms, muscled from the endless swinging of heavy tools, were pocked with burn scars. Varick didn't have the stamina. His arms, she knew, were strong, but his breath didn't last. He would never be more than a helper. When the forger tired of him, the boy would go elsewhere, perhaps to the smelting furnace where they melted the iron ore. Maybe he could offer himself to help work the huge bellows that kept the furnace fires ablaze. Or, Estrild thought, perhaps his smile and jaunty good cheer would seem of some value to the men and they would use him to run errands and deliver messages.

He had been her friend from the time she was very young. He had been often alone, because the boys his age, as they grew, played rough games and mocked him when he couldn't keep up. Estrild, aware of the boy's loneliness, had brought him little gifts: flowers, sometimes, that she picked in the meadow, wilting and crumpled in her small hands. He had always pretended to her that they were gifts of value, had hugged and thanked her, and once he had taught her to weave blossoms into a wreath for her head.

It was Varick who had explained the finch's skeleton to her and had taught her the bird calls, too: which was which—the throaty trill of the warblers, the chirr and cheep of the nightingale, and the harsh scream of the brown owl that nested in the rocks at the edge of the bog.

Thinking of the owl now as the last small goat pulled loose from her and pranced away, she glanced toward the bog, which loomed dark behind the thicket of growth at the edge of the village. No birds in there. Birds liked the meadow borders, where insects twitched and hopped in the tall grasses. From his nest, at night, the owl could hear the field mice and rabbits that were his prey; he swooped through the open spaces and dove between the crops to make his kill.

But the bog was still and dank, with an unhealthy smell to it, and on darkest nights, mysterious glowing lights appeared in the thick air. Estrild had seen them, flickering there; people called them evil spirits and warned their children not to go near. Varick laughed at her and said there was nothing to be afraid of, that the lights were caused by the gassy air that rose from the bog, that they were nothing more than tiny flashes of lightning, a special kind that came from the earth instead of the sky. But she noticed that when Varick entered the bog to cut peat for the iron-forger's fire, he did it only at midday, and did not venture deep.

"I get dirty enough in the village," he explained. "I don't need bog mud pasted all over my legs as well.

"If you go too deep in, the bog sucks at your feet," he added. He made sucking, slurping sounds with his mouth, and laughed.

But she was unable to laugh with him. The thought of the clammy, ill-smelling bog grabbing her bare feet and pulling her down was too frightening. She'd heard stories. Oh, maybe they were imaginary stories—Estrild didn't know—but people spoke of those who had disappeared: an animal escaped from its pen, a runaway child, or an ancient grandfather whose mind wandered and caused his legs to do the same. Gone. Into the bog and never seen again.

"You be careful," she had scolded Varick, but he grinned and rolled his eyes at her, dismissive of her fears.

The goats played, bleating, butting each other and scampering in the pen. She spoke to them affectionately, calling them by names she had given them herself: *Jumpy, Short-tail, Smiler.* Then she picked up the heavy milk container and covered it with a cloth to keep the bugs away. Women's work, milking. She yearned to be out in the field, guiding the ox, or over in the sacred grove where her father and many of the other men were today, beginning to prepare the festival area so that the druids could invoke the gods and bring another year's prosperity to the village. Or— this most of all, Estrild thought, remembering again the loss of the uncle who had loved her—she yearned to be sharpening her sword and preparing for battle. Facing the tribe's enemies, she knew, would not bring him back. But proving her own worth on the battlefield might in some way avenge his death.

On the path she encountered her friends Gudrun and Thora, sisters near her age, laughing as they followed a noisy wing-flapping goose to the pond. They dragged a small cart piled with dirty clothing. "Come with us!" they invited her. "We'll net some fish while we do the washing!"

Estrild was tempted. The early dawn had been chilly, but now the sun was out and it was going to be a warm day. It would feel good to leave her shoes on the bank and splash in the shallow edge of the pond. And fish? Though she rarely had much luck catching anything, it was fun trying. She hesitated, then shook her head.

"I have to get the milk home," she explained, indicating the container she carried.

Gudrun nodded. "Your mum needs it," she said. "You tell her that. Tell her Gudrun said."

Thora, the lighthearted one, laughed at her sister's seriousness and mimicked her. *"Gudrun said, Gudrun said . . ."*

Estrild ignored Thora. "I'll tell her," she replied. Gudrun was young, still, but she was apprenticed to the midwife and took it seriously. When the new baby began to come, probably her friend would be there to help.

"It'll be soon," Gudrun reminded her.

"I know. But not right away. She'll be at the festival."

Thora twirled in a circle and her long hair flew around her. The goose squawked and waddled forward, startled by the girl's impetuous dance. "Don't you love the festival?" Thora exclaimed. "All the food!"

"I love that part," Estrild acknowledged. "The celebrations. And the bard, with his branch and bells." Always, as he entered the grove, the bard carried and shook a metal branch adorned with bells, to announce his arrival and alert the village to his performance of lengthy songs.

"Do you not love the druids?" Thora asked mischievously. She pulled a wadded cloth from the cart, draped it over her head like a druid's hood, and intoned some ominous, woeful sounds.

Estrild laughed. But Gudrun looked nervously

around and told her sister to stop. It seemed dangerous to mock the priests.

Thora tossed the cloth back in the cart. "I love
all of it," she said, "even the druids. Except when
they . . . you know."

"When they make the sacrifice?" Estrild said.

Thora nodded. "Yes, I don't like the blood. And
the way the lambs and goats cry out," she added.

"They're only animals," Gudrun pointed out
matter-of-factly.

Thora held out her woven skirt and twirled again.
She hummed a melody to accompany her impromptu
dance.

Estrild smiled, watching her, but she thought
of the goats she called Smiler and Jumpy, and the
others. They were only animals, it was true, but she
agreed with Thora. She did not want to see them
with their stretched necks held to the stone, awaiting
the knife.

Her friends had not spoken of the part of the ceremony when the new warriors were named. Estrild
didn't mention it either. But the manhood ritual

would surprise her friends this year. This spring the ritual would be different. Her excitement was mounting.

There had been a shift in the mood of the village as the moon slowly swelled its way toward full. The new leaves began to open on the trees, and the starkness of the limbs interlaced against the sky changed to a breeze-tossed shifting pattern of pale green. Small children now ran and laughed on the paths after a winter of confinement in smoke-filled dwellings. Mothers proudly displayed their new infants born during the winter; the wee ones squinted and blinked in light brighter than anything they had yet seen.

Her mother, as she had promised, had taken the intricate fabric from the loom. Now and then Estrild looked at it, folded on a shelf, waiting for its edges to be fringed, and marveled at its colors. Many of the tribe's women dyed their wool from time to time, but it made the process much longer and more difficult; most clothing was colorless, undyed, except for the ceremonial costumes or the tunics that the greatest warriors wore into battle. And none she remembered had such a complicated pattern of such varied colors. Briefly, admiring the fabric, she had considered how she would look, wrapped in such a magnificent shawl. She had fingered her long hair, imagining it decorated with blossoms. But after a moment she found that her fingers were twisting her hair, pulling it to the side and upward, and she reminded herself that very soon Varick would teach her to make the Suebian knot, the complex twist that adorned the heads of warriors.

From his special hut near the druids' longhouse, she had overheard the bard rehearsing. His songs were of their history and told of past battles and triumphs. Several lads stayed there with him, learning, so that the songs would continue as they always had; bards grew old and died as all people would, but the songs and tales would have new life with each generation.

Her father and the other men had been returning tired each evening from the sacred grove. When the time came, when the entire tribe gathered there, it would be groomed to perfection: every blade of grass trimmed, rocks smoothed and polished, the stone altar spotless, tables constructed and carved posts placed to outline the ceremonial areas.

Estrild watched the moon. Her mother did as well, knowing that her eleventh labor would begin when, after the coming fullness, it was next a new sliver. Estrild watched, though, because it would be at the full moon, the time of the ceremony, when thanks was given for the harvest and the new young warriors were presented, that she would be among them, announcing herself as the new holder of her uncle Erhard's shield. On that day she would be claiming her place—and the place of all females—in the world.

She and Varick continued the exercises, chanting and stomping, dawn after dawn. If the iron-forger knew, he said nothing, as long as the boy was there and ready to work when the sun was up.

The shield Varick used at their practice, the one that would be presented to Ralf when the time came, changed day by day. The forger was creating intricate designs on it. Estrild had felt the early curved lines, and now the complicated swirls and circles formed the shape of leaves, with precious stones embedded in the pattern. Ralf's father was a wealthy man, with slaves and a large herd of cattle. Most shields were decorated; Estrild had seen them at the ceremonies, and the one she was using in the practice sessions was embossed with curved lines. But Ralf's, when it was completed, would be unique, its design more complex, more beautiful than those of the most distinguished warriors.

It was too dark in the predawn to see details, but she ran her fingers over the raised pattern and marveled at it. "It's beautiful. But why?" she asked Varick. "Why will Ralf have a shield so magnificent?"

"His father," Varick explained with a shrug. "Do you know Ralf's father?"

"No."

Varick shook his head. "He's a braggart."

"Like Ralf," Estrild replied, laughing.

"And he wants his son to be special. Better than the other new warriors," Varick went on. "He's paying the iron-forger many, many coins for this." He stroked the configurations of the shield. "Feel how light it is, too. It's partly bronze." He handed it to her.

"Well," Estrild said, after she had lifted and felt the lightness of it, "I'm going to use my uncle's. It's very plain, and heavy." She fell silent for a moment, thinking suddenly: *And stained with his blood.* She gave the decorated shield back to Varick and picked up her own borrowed one again. "But I'll be just as good a warrior as Ralf," she said. "I'll be *better* than Ralf."

Then she glanced at Varick with uncertainty. "I will, won't I?" she asked.

"If you practice," he told her, and she could see, even in the dim light, that he was smiling. "And now it's time for something new," he added.

"The knot!" Estrild, without thinking, touched her hair.

"That'll be soon. But for now: look!" He picked up the large goatskin bag he had brought with him this morning and reached inside. "We're going to start practicing with swords."

She took the one he offered and felt its smooth hilt.

"We'll practice lunging forward with it," he explained, but then warned, "Be careful, though, not to touch it to the shield. The forger would notice the marks."

She nodded. She knew too well about the marks a sword could make; her uncle's shield, dented and scarred by countless sword and spear thrusts and darkened with his blood, hung against one wall of their dwelling, in a place of honor. It was a talisman for Estrild. From time to time she had watched her mother touch the shield and murmur a prayer. She, too, touched Erhard's shield now and then with sadness and respect. But her own murmur was not one of religion. It was a vow of vengeance.

Later, making her way home at sunrise, Estrild found herself shifting her weight and thrusting her arms forward, one at a time. Her breath came in short woofs as she rehearsed the charge and thrust that might, in times of real battle, plunge a sword into the enemy. She could still feel the outline, in her palm, of the sword's hilt. It had been too large, actually, for her hand.

Perhaps, when the time was right, after she had taken her place among the warriors, the iron-forger could make her a smaller, but even deadlier, sword.

It seemed, lately, that she encountered Ralf more often than she ever had before. The village population was small, so everyone was known to one another. There were no strangers at the ceremonies, only neighbors and cousins and familiar tradesmen; they had celebrated marriages together and mourned one another's dead. Still, Ralf was older than Estrid. He had not been a playmate during earlier years. He had always been part of the boisterous and swaggering group of future warriors who ignored the younger children and had rarely crossed her path. Until now. Now, suddenly, she seemed to see him everywhere.

He was at the pond, smirking at her, when she carried the cooking pot there to wash it. And he was at the edge of the newly plowed field when she went to call her brothers for dinner.

"Got enough food for me, too?" he asked her then, but there was not a joking feel to it. He had a spiteful look. Then he added, "Or are you eating the extra, plumping yourself up, building strength?"

Estrild looked at the ground and didn't reply. But she wondered, returning home, what he had meant.

Later, she was walking with her friend Thora in the afternoon on the path beside the sheep-shearing shed, from which they could hear the bustle and the bleats of the frightened animals as their thick winter wool was carved away. Suddenly there was Ralf once again. He didn't speak. But when they passed each other, he made a succession of harsh sounds under his breath behind a cupped hand.

"What was *that*?" Thora asked, as they continued on. "He sounded like our cow, the one whose calf died! *What happened to my calf?*" she bellowed, cow-like, and laughed.

Estrild chuckled, pretending to her companion that it was funny. But it wasn't. She knew it wasn't, because she recognized the sound that Ralf had made and aimed at her. It was the warriors' chant. It was *barritas*.

She said nothing to her friend. Later she looked for Varick, to question and accuse him. But the forge was unoccupied, its fire smoldering and the tools set aside.

"Where is the forger?" she asked some villagers who were nearby.

"He's down at the grove," a nearby child told her, looking up from the ground where he was poking a half-dead mouse with a twig. "They needed him to help set the altar."

"Is Varick with him?"

The child scratched at an insect bite on his neck until it bled, then sucked the blood from his thumb. He stared at her.

"Varick. You know. The boy who helps him."

"He went to the longhouse," the child muttered, finally, and pointed up the hill toward the place where the druids lived and studied together.

"Why?"

The child shrugged. "They wanted him for work

that needed doing. Maybe they'll give him a coin. And the forger was gone, anyway.

"You could give me a coin, couldn't you, for telling you?"

Estrild ignored his outstretched hand and turned away from the boy, who made a face and went back to torturing the mouse.

She hesitated. It was time for her to go home. She knew her mother expected her there to tend the little ones so she could rest before the preparations for the evening meal. And she didn't really want to go near the longhouse. She never felt comfortable there. The druids, with their robes, their faces shadowed by hoods, were aloof and separate, murmuring to one another, savoring their power. They were both priests and judges. And all of them men.

"Why are there no women druids?" she had asked her mother once.

Her mother had looked startled, shocked. "It's not our role," she said. Then she lowered her voice, even though they were together in the dwelling with no others there but the little ones. "I heard once that there was a druidess in some other place. But I don't think it's true. It's not our role to judge. And women don't have the visions. We can't see what the entrails tell. Or the birds."

"I can," Estrild had replied haughtily. "I know exactly what the birds are telling me. When they fly in great swarms from the south, they're saying, *Winter is over*."

Her mother had laughed and nodded in agreement. "But the druids learn more than that from the birds," she pointed out. "They watch the patterns, the way they swoop. It's all omens. No one can read the omens but the druids."

"A woman could learn to," Estrild argued.

"And the entrails?"

Estrild made a face and her mother laughed. "I know. When I slice open a goat or a lamb, I just see the mess, and of course the parts I'll cook, like the liver. But the druids! When they sacrifice the animal, all the knowledge is there, in the entrails, for them to see and sort and understand. A woman doesn't have that special power."

"A woman *could*, if they would let her," Estrild argued, but her mother had shaken her head and turned away, her attention on household things.

She resented the druids, that they excluded females, and she feared them a little, with their greater knowledge and their shrouded costumes, their dark incantations. But right now she wanted to find Varick. So she headed toward the longhouse.

And there he was, just emerging from the large door. He saw Estrild, waved cheerfully, and came toward her. "Look!" he called. "They gave me a coin!" He held it up to show her. "All I had to do was hammer and bend the dents out of their collars, for the ceremony." The druids wore wide, decorated gold collars on ceremonial occasions. But gold was a soft metal and easily marred.

Estrild didn't return his greeting. She was upset.

"You *told*," she accused him.

"Told what?"

"Ralf. He knows."

Varick paused, puzzled. "Ralf? I haven't talked to him at all. I *never* talk to Ralf or his friends. They shoved me out of their group when I was little because I couldn't run fast. He bloodied my nose once when I was about five."

"How could he know about what I'm doing, then? But he does. I'm sure of it. He follows me, and murmurs things."

They began walking toward the forger's shed, and the path to Estrild's house beyond it. "I don't know," Varick replied. "Except—" He hesitated.

"What?"

"When you and I finished the other morning, and went back just as the sun was starting to rise, you asked me about the knot, remember?"

Her hand went to her hair. "Yes. I've asked and asked you about it, and when you'd teach me how to do it. And you said soon."

He nodded. "You were impatient."

"I still am," she pointed out. "You've been promising for days."

Varick ignored her comment. "And when I left you that morning and turned off to go to the forge, you called after me."

They stopped walking. They were at that same place now, the place where they always separated. "I did," Estrild said. "I called that I needed time to practice it, and you called back that I should start combing my hair and get the snarls and snags out of it, so that—"

"So that I could show you how to make the knot. But we should have remembered to be quieter. The forger heard me call to you."

Oh, no. They had tried to be so careful. No one had known of their predawn meetings.

"What did he say?"

"Wanted to know where I'd been, but didn't give me a chance to answer, just grumbled that I was always going off for a piss when there was work to be done. Then he asked me where the new shield was, the one for Ralf. Ralf's father was there, wanting to see it."

Estrild held her breath. "What did you tell him?"

"It was lucky that I had stopped and put it in my storage shed after I left you, along with the swords. Remember, that's where I was headed when we called to each other about the knot."

"Yes, and—?"

"I told him I'd go get it, and I did. I brought it to him, and they looked at it together. Ralf's father said he wanted more decoration around the top edge."

"So you didn't say anything about me." She was relieved.

Varick fell silent. Then he explained, "Just as he was leaving, Ralf's father asked what girl had been wanting to know about the knot. He had heard our voices. I said it was you, that it was the leather-worker's daughter, but that you were just curious because your little brother wanted you to do it with his hair, just for play, but you didn't know how."

"And he believed you?"

"I think so. He didn't ask any more."

Estrild didn't reply. From where she stood, she could see cooking smoke wafting from the chimney holes in the thatched roofs of the dwellings. The working day was ending. Her mother would be angry that she was so late. And now she was angry at herself, for having called to Varick about the knot, for having forgotten the need for secrecy in that early morning moment. She felt certain now that Ralf's father had said something about her to his son, and that Ralf himself, appearing now so often at the places where she was, as if he was seeking her out, was trying to find out what she was up to.

She turned away from Varick and ran down the path toward home.

"Come to the field in the morning. It's time for planting."

Her older brother Carolus, reaching past Estrild for another helping of boiled meat, was talking to her younger sisters. They pouted, preferring to spend their daytime hours at play, but it was, as he said, time, and helping to plant the seeds was their task.

"I wish we had slaves," Hilda said with a pout.

"Yes, why can't we have slaves?" Lotte, her twin, whined, nodding in agreement.

"More mouths to feed?" their father replied gruffly. "We don't need slaves."

"A girl slave could help Mother."

"Estrild helps your mother. Be quiet." Their father

rose from his eating bench and readied himself to leave. In the evenings, after the meal, he and the other men gathered for ale and jokes and bragging. Carolus and Alard, warriors already, both so close to true manhood, joined him now.

The seed from last fall's harvest had been stored over the winter. In the morning the twins would fill aprons that were tied around them and walk barefoot through the rutted furrows the plow had dug, sprinkling the seed that would create next year's grain. Later they would chase the birds away from the new seedlings, and then they would help to weed the field throughout the summer.

The grain fed the animals all winter and provided the flour from which their bread was made. It was Estrild's job, each day, to place an apronful on the quern, lift the heavy upper grindstone into place and turn its wooden handle until the grain was hulled and crushed. By midsummer they would add crushed berries to the bread and it would be a welcome treat, the sweetness. But now, in spring, no berries were yet ripe. It seemed endless, endless, the creating of their meals.

Her mother would help in the field after the new baby had arrived, following and instructing the twins, wearing the infant in a sack tied to her chest and keeping an eye, as Estrild did too, on the mischievous toddlers who would scamper and play at the edge of the nearby path.

It was true that in the larger fields belonging to the more prosperous men of the village, slaves did much of the work. The same battle in which her uncle had died had brought with it the capture of new slaves; watching the returning procession, Estrild had seen the captives, roped together, defeated and sullen. Later she would see them in the village and the field, hard at work, beaten for transgressions. But rarely did a slave run away. Those who tried were caught and hanged without a trial, their bodies dragged to the bog.

One female slave, taken when she was very young, had grown to become beautiful, with a quick wit, easy laugh, and great charm. Eventually she had been freed to wed a young man of the village. Estrild had heard her story often because the villagers liked to recount it. But the woman herself, the former slave, was elderly now, her beauty gone and her body thickened from childbearing and years of heavy work. Hearing her speak, one could perceive still the slight accent that had stayed with her from her childhood tribe. Estrild wondered what her memories were. Had she had a mother, left behind to mourn? Did she yearn to go back to her own people? Or had she turned to her new husband with hope, savoring her freedom, looking ahead to taking a respected place in village life, only to find herself doomed to the same chores?

After her father and brothers had gone, the little ones were settled onto their sleeping mats, the twins wiped the pots and plates and set them on the shelves, and Estrild helped her mother pull the heavy chain that lifted the cooking pot away from the fire. Then she went outside to milk the goats again. On her way, she took the carved wooden comb that hung from an iron nail on the wall near the door. Walking to the goat pen, she began to pull the comb through her tangled hair.

※

"Now. *Finally*." Estrild's tone reminded Varick that she had been waiting impatiently for this.

They were whispering. Varick's encounter with Ralf's father had made them both wary. They kept their voices low, and this morning, on the path to the clearing where they always practiced, they had peered through the dark across the grass on both sides, alert to the darting movements of animals, wondering if something human might be watching them in the predawn.

His arms were empty today. No shields, no swords.

And she carried only the comb.

In the darkness, he fingered her hair. "Good," he said approvingly. "No tangles."

"It took a while. And it hurt."

He laughed. "That's why I never comb my hair," he said. "Turn your back to me." She did so.

"Now, hold still," he ordered.

She did, and he raked through her waist-long hair with the comb, then handed the comb back to her.

"Have you ever made a knot for yourself?" she asked him.

He laughed. "My hair's too snarled. I don't even have a comb. Anyway, if I tried to have a knot, even just pretending, the young warriors would turn on me. They gave me bloodied noses just for fun when I was a little boy. But they'd do it out of anger now, if they saw me with a knot."

Then he added, confessing, "Actually, I've done it sometimes, at night, when no one's nearby. Just to feel what it would be like. That's how I know how."

He was smoothing and separating her hair.

"Does it matter which side?" she asked.

He had pulled all of her hair to the left side of her head, and held it there now, grasping it with one hand. "I don't think so," he told her. "You've seen them. They use both."

"Some of them put it on the very top," she pointed out.

"The older warriors," he said. "I think in the old days they did it that way to make themselves seem taller. But the boys? The young warriors? They mostly put it here, above the ear." He nudged the place on her head.

"Do it there, then," she told him. Then she asked, "Do you have something in your mouth? Your voice sounds—"

Still clutching her hair with his left hand, he brought his other hand to his mouth, withdrew something, and held it close to her face so that she could see. "I grabbed it when we passed the willow tree where the path curves. It's good and strong, but I put it in my mouth to moisten it. We need it to tie your hair at the end. Otherwise it will all fall apart."

She could see the length of strong, pliable willow shoot that he held. "I'll get more," she said, "so that I'll have it when I'm doing this by myself."

He returned the willow to his mouth, and both hands went to work.

"What are you doing now?" she asked him.

"Separating it into two sections," he explained. "You'll have to practice this. It might be hard at first, but your fingers will figure it out." He moved away from her, holding the two thick sections of her hair, and began to twist them together, over and under, in and out.

"You can do this braiding part," he assured her. "I've seen you comb your sisters' hair and braid flower blossoms in for decoration."

She nodded and he said, "Hold still."

"Sorry."

He chuckled and his hands continued to move, holding the entwined hair firmly as he worked toward the end.

"I should have brought grease. Can you find some when you're doing it yourself?" he asked. "It will go together more easily for you if you grease the hair first."

"My father rubs the leathers with animal fat to soften them," she said. "Would that do?"

"Perfect. You don't need much," he said, talking as his fingers moved deftly. "Just rub a little through the hair before you start to coil it around itself."

"I made a belt for my father out of strips of leather, braided," she told him, "and he had the forger make a buckle for it."

"I remember that! It was a fine bronze buckle."

"Yes, he wears that belt every day."

He moved away from her, holding the intertwined rope of hair. "There," he said. "I'll tie it now." Holding the end with one hand, he used the other to take the willow strip from his mouth and wound it tightly several times around the braid, then fastened it securely.

"Now what?" she asked.

"Now we make the knot with it."

It was still dark. She twisted herself and strained to see, without success. But she could feel the motions of his hands. "I'm just making a loop," he explained. "Now I'm going to take the end and thread it through the loop and pull it tight."

She felt his hands guiding the braid into a spiral shape and then pulling the end though.

He let go. "Move your head," he told her, and she did. The knot held firm.

"Good," he said. "After it's all knotted, then the hair tries to unwind, and it actually firms it up."

"Can I touch it?"

"Of course."

She reached up and felt the complex knot, its whorls and twists, coiled tight and firm above her left ear. In the dark, she smiled.

"I wish I could leave it there," she said.

"No!" he said, alarmed at the suggestion. "They'd—"

Estrild laughed. "I know, I know. I won't. Why don't you take it apart now? Then let me try to make it myself."

He did. Then, gradually, awkwardly, she learned to make the warrior's knot by herself. On the tree line at the edge of the bog, the sky began to lighten in the dawn.

"May I have this?" Estrild asked her mother. She held up the narrow strip of colorful woven fabric that was hanging from a twig at the edge of the wooden loom. The much larger piece of cloth, the finished shawl from which this small piece had been snipped, was folded now, fringed and waiting for the occasion when Estrild would envelop herself in its bright colors.

"Why? I thought I'd use it to tie the swaddle around the new baby." Her mother looked up from the surface where she was shaping the day's bread.

"I want to give someone a gift. This would be a good way for him to tie back his hair. He never has had anything nice."

"Who?"

"The boy named Varick," Estrild told her. "The one who helps at the forge."

"Varick? I knew his mother. I remember when she died. People thought it would be better if the baby was just tossed into the grave with her, but his father said no, and named him, and kept him alive. But then his father died a while after, and no one wanted the boy. He's very sickly. Why do you want to give him a gift?"

Estrild shrugged. "Because he's never had one," she said. "And he gave me a bird skeleton. I want to make a clasp out of it when I have time.

"Varick knows everything about birds," she added.

"He should be a druid," her mother said, laughing. She turned the loaf over, shaped it with her strong hands, and handed it to Estrild. "Here. This one's ready for the oven. And yes," she said. "You may give the piece of cloth to Varick.

"When you do? Tell him his mother was a good woman," she added.

The moon was swelling now, and the damp air was warmer. Rain fell occasionally, and they were glad of it. The seeds had been planted. The crops would depend upon the sun that would warm the earth as well as the moisture that would engorge the new growth as it lifted from its fragile, threadlike roots.

Spring brought a hum of energy to the village, a feeling of *soon*. On her sleeping mat, in the dark, Estrild formed the knot again and again until she could do it quickly, her hands separating and twisting and coiling without thought. She was careful not to let herself fall asleep with the knot intact. No one must see it; no one must know.

She began to plan.

When the day came . . . soon, soon . . . everyone in the village would be up early. They would clean themselves. Most had not bathed for many months. But at this time of renewal—a time when the gods would look upon them, would judge them, would decide their future—the people would be washed and wearing new, or at least newly clean, garments. Estrild's father and older brothers would leave the dwelling early. Her father had duties to perform at the sacred grove and the boys would be joining up with their special group of warriors. She and her mother would prepare their food and see them off at daybreak.

Estrild would feed and milk the goats as always; animals could not go unmilked. The twins would take hay from the stack and toss it to the ox and the horse. The pig would wallow in her pen and gulp the scraps tossed her way, and her piglets would wrestle each other and climb their mother's belly for a chance at her milk.

Then—this was the part she wanted to make firm in her mind—when the chanting from the longhouse began, when the people began moving toward the grove, she and her mother would take the smallest two by their hands, and the twins would follow along, and they would join the crowd. Estrild would be wearing her new shawl wrapped around her, and her mother would be glancing to see if other women noticed and admired the intricately woven fabric, how unusual it was, how brightly colored.

They would gather, then. Her father would be standing already with the men. Carolus and Alard would be with their group of younger warriors. Estrild's mother, with her children, would make her way to the group of women and children on the other side, the place they had been assigned, as women always were, on the outskirts. The entire population of the village would be gathered in the grove, all but the young boys who had been chosen to become new warriors. That group would be waiting together, unseen, hidden in a copse of thick trees, nervously boasting to each other, waiting for the time of their ceremonial entrance.

After everyone had gathered, the sound of the prayer chant would begin from the distance as the druids approached. Estrild remembered, from earlier years, how the villagers fell silent then. Even the smallest of children were hushed and in awe.

That was the moment, she planned, the time when the druids were on their way to the grove, when the people had turned, reverential, to watch the slow procession of hooded and robed priests, that she would whisper to the twins, "Watch Bruno and Birta. I forgot something." She would turn the toddlers over to her sisters and slip away through the crowd. No one would notice.

Then: quickly, quickly! All the eyes would be on the solemn parade of druids, none on Estrild as she would make her way soundlessly in the other direction, out of the grove and back to the dwelling. There she would shed the shawl and the simple dress she wore beneath it, folding them both quickly (in her mind, in the planning) and then slipping into the tunic she had hidden, an old one outgrown by a brother. Next her practiced hands would part her hair and make the Suebian knot that said to the world: *warrior.* Finally she would carefully lift her uncle's shield from its place on the wall, and she would take up his spear. Then, garbed and armed and ready and proud, she would make her way back to the edge of the grove and take her place with the boys who waited to be called forward.

She rehearsed and rehearsed it all in her mind. Her father turned in his sleep, and snored. Nearer by, one of the twins cried out briefly from a dream, then fell back into a deep slumber. Estrild smoothed her hair, breathed deeply, and counted to herself the number of nights left until her life, and perhaps the lives of all the girls in her village, including her younger sisters and females yet to be born, would change.

Don't expect, her mother had said, often. But she had. Night after night Estrild had lain on her mat, planning, expecting. Dawn upon dawn she had gone to the meadow to learn and practice. In her mind she had prepared for this day, had reviewed how she would proceed during each minute of it, and imagined the triumph it would be. The excitement, the anticipation, of it had made her wakeful. Now the time of the full moon was here. And she was ready.

But suddenly she felt uneasy. Something seemed askew.

She wondered: Were there omens, warnings that things would go wrong? Clouds had slid across the full moon as it rose. But didn't clouds often travel through the sky? There had been a shriek from the edge of the bog: a small animal, certainly, grabbed by an owl; it happened often, and yet—was this cry different? A portent? One of her sisters, the twin named Lotte, had stumbled yesterday and fallen against a sharp stone as she ran home from the pond. They had to hold her down while her mother sewed the wound closed and wrapped it tightly in cloth. Such accidents took place all the time. Was there reason to think this time ominous? And a long V of birds had crossed, high but not so high that their squawking cries weren't heard, over the village yesterday morning just as the sun began to rise. Had that meant something? Did not birds traverse the sky every dawn?

She couldn't remember. That, too: that odd, sudden little lapse of everyday memory—was it something to note? Surely not. Estrild shook off the feeling of unease that afflicted her when she woke.

Nothing was amiss, she reassured herself. It was only excitement that she felt. Anticipation.

Her father and brothers left very early, as she had expected. Men and boys, she reflected again, seemed always to be given the more important roles. Her mother, she knew, would argue that to cook, to prepare the food, to birth the babies and feed and clean them, to make the garments they all wore, to help in the fields: all of that was just as important. But it wasn't. No one cheered for them or sang them off to battle. No one placed laurels of victory around their necks. No one—

Estrild's thoughts were interrupted by Lotte, who was up from her mat now and complaining loudly that the stitched-up gash on her leg ached, that it hurt too much to go out and feed the animals, that Hilda should do it alone this morning, that she would need a heavy stick to lean on in order to walk. "*Go,*" their mother said sternly, and pointed to the door. "You're fine. Do your chores. We must hurry this morning."

Then she leaned over with a sudden grunt of discomfort, put her own hand on her back, and sighed. "I hope this one isn't coming early."

Estrild looked up from spooning gruel into the mouths of the two little ones. "Are you having birthing pains?" she asked anxiously. *Please say no*, she thought. If her mother had to stay in the dwelling, if her birthing time had started . . . would the midwife even come? And miss the spring ceremony? If she didn't? What then? All of Estrild's careful plans would be ruined.

"No. Sometimes there are early pains, but they're only warnings. I'm fine. It'll be soon: with the new moon, I'm guessing." Her mother took a deep breath and stood straight. "Listen!" she said, tilting her head.

From the distance now, from the longhouse, Estrild could hear the muted chanting of the druids begin. Hastily her mother raised the cooking pot and fixed its chain. From the open door she called to the twins to come quickly. She went to the shelf, reached for the folded shawl, and handed it to her daughter. "It's starting," she said. "We must ready ourselves."

"I forgot something," Estrild whispered to the twins. "Here. Hold Bruno's hand. I have to go back to the dwelling. I won't be long." She transferred the toddler's hand to Lotte's and turned to find her way through the throng.

Her mother didn't notice. She was squeezed between two other women, and her eyes were fixed on the approaching druids, who swayed in their robes as they began to intone the spring prayers. The incantations would be very lengthy, Estrild knew. They prayed to all the gods, especially Nerthus, who oversaw the earth's fertility, and offered thanks. They recited lengthy exhortations for rain—but gentle rain, not torrents nor floods—and for sun and gentle winds, for the bees to be healthy, the cows and goats abundant with milk, for no sickness to fall upon the village, for the tool blades to be sharp, the arrows true, the forest thick with stags, and the village well water to be clear and deep.

Two lambs, tied to a post near the altar, cried for their mothers.

Estrild pushed through the crowd. "Sorry," she murmured as she forced her way past people who had their eyes closed, trance-like, listening to the druids. They were startled and annoyed at the interruption but stepped aside to let her pass. One woman noticed the colorful shawl and touched it with a quick, admiring smile.

Behind her, she could hear the druids calling out the names of the god Tuisto and his son Mannus, and other gods; she hurried on and had already removed the shawl as she entered the family dwelling.

Quickly, quickly, now, as she had rehearsed in her mind: she placed the shawl back on the shelf, folded her discarded clothing, and slipped into the boy's tunic. Next, the knot. She reached for the small container of grease that she had kept hidden under her mat. Her fingers, so practiced now, pulled the length of hair, teased and separated and twisted it, then coiled it back upon itself above her left ear. She shook her head to assess its firmness. Yes! It held tight. She was marked, now: *warrior.* And from the grove she could hear the chanting continue.

Preparing to return to the ceremony, now as her new self, Estrild snatched up a small animal hide, something her father had brought back from his leatherworks. It fell into place over her shoulder. Next, she took a deep breath, lifted her uncle's shield from its place of honor on the wall, and stood silently, remembering him. Finally, after a moment, she picked up the spear that had long stood beside the shield. She felt herself change, then. She was not a thin, unfinished girl any longer. From today onward she would always be *Estrild, First Woman Warrior*.

She left the dwelling and hurried back down the now deserted path, this time heading not toward the crowd where her mother still stood with the children and other women, not toward the grouped men and boys on the opposite side. She went instead to the trees that bordered the grove, the place where the new warriors waited, concealed.

She pushed aside some thick bushes with the spear and inserted herself silently into the group. The nearby waiting boys shifted their space to make room, perplexed and annoyed by the late arrival.

Then they peered more closely in confusion. With a feeling of satisfaction, she realized that she looked like one of them. She was small, it was true, but there were other young warriors who were slight of build. Her shield was scarred and stained, and the boys' shields were mostly new, but she felt a fierce pride in grasping her uncle's weaponry. She could see Ralf holding his highly decorated one with a smug sort of vanity. From his nearby spot he glanced at her briefly as she slipped into the group. He turned away at first, then looked back quickly, in recognition. His gaze was hostile.

A piercing cry interrupted the chanted prayers, and though she couldn't see from behind the thick trees where she stood, she perceived that a lamb had now been sacrificed. The murmuring of the druids became louder and she knew that now they were sorting through the warm spilled innards and calling out the omens. Next: frightened bleating and a second agonized cry, followed by more pronouncements from the druids. Then, finally, a joyful murmur swept through the crowd. The villagers had been assured of the satisfaction of the gods; they had been promised a fruitful summer and bountiful crops to come.

She pushed aside a branch, leaned forward, and peered into the grove, trying to remember exactly what would come next. It would be the trials. The druids stepped aside then, and the Council, the leaders of the village, would act as judges. If crimes had been committed, or accusations made, the prisoners would be brought before them now. Slaves who had tried to run away would be put to death, but that was unlikely this spring. There were no new slaves, and those who had been captured earlier were by now resigned to live their lives here in servitude.

Death was not a frequent penalty. One spring in the past, Estrild remembered, a wife had been accused of being unfaithful to her husband. She was brought forward, and some of the villagers had called out that she should die. But the Council appointed the woman's husband to judge her. He came forward, stripped her of her clothing, and used his sharp knife to shave the hair from her head. Then she was publicly flogged. Estrild recalled holding on

to her mother's skirt and hiding her eyes as the flog-
ging was administered.

Today the transgressions presented to the Council were smaller ones. She listened as two men
came forward and presented their arguments over
a gambling debt. It seemed to Estrild a very small
thing, but the pair was angry, each accusing the
other. The Councilors heeded them both, one after
the other, then huddled to talk among themselves.
It didn't take long. From where she stood in the
trees, she couldn't hear the verdict, but she watched
as the decision was explained to the two men, who
listened, nodded, and then returned to their places
in the crowd.

Two other men came forward next and presented their dispute over land; they had been quar-
reling over the boundaries of a field. The Councilors
listened again and asked questions. Estrild felt both
bored and impatient. She thought about what was to
come. Beyond the throngs, on the edge of the grove,
she could see the tables laden with food and pitch-
ers of drink. The feasting would happen at the end,

after the ceremony of new warriors, and the rest of the afternoon would be taken up with the celebratory eating, drinking, and entertainment. The bard would appear with his silver branch of bells and would sing his lengthy tales of heroism and tragedy from the past. There would be spritely music, and dancing. Congratulations would be bestowed. She felt a glow of excitement mixed with apprehension. She was not accustomed to being the center of attention, and today that would be her role. In her lengthy rehearsals at night, she had included that part: how she would nod and smile and accept the astonished good wishes from the villagers—and especially, she knew, from the women. Today would mark a new time in the lives of girls and women, and she, Estrild, would be the center of it, the *maker* of it. But she was ready for this. Varick had told her she was ready.

The Councilors droned on, asking questions about who had built the fence, whose cow had eaten of which grasses, through how many moons had this dispute gone unresolved.

She could tell that the young men surrounding her, boys she had known since childhood, were impatient as well. They shifted their weight, adjusted their shields, and she could hear some of them rehearsing their *barritas* under their breath. All of them waiting in the trees were eager for these tedious land dispute proceedings to conclude so that the next—and final—part of the day could begin. She had watched it each spring from the crowd, had watched as the young boys, new warriors, self-conscious but proud, moved forward, thumping their spears against the ground, intoning the *barritas* behind their raised shields. They would move in formation to the center of the grove, the space before the altar, and fall silent, facing both the Council and the druids. Then they would step forward, one at a time, as their names were announced. The druids would intone the name and the Council, with one voice, would add the title: Warrior. The crowd would cheer.

Estrild felt some movement to her left. She lowered her shield a bit and glanced to her side. Ralf had shoved himself past two others and appeared there, next to her, suddenly. He looked angry.

"It's not too late," he whispered harshly. "Get out of our group."

She straightened her shoulders and faced him. "I'm staying," she whispered back, "and next year there will be more of us. More girls."

A murmur suddenly went through the boys:

"Get ready."

"Get ready."

They all stood straighter. In the grove, the two arguing men were now listening to the decision of their judges. In a moment they would return to their places in the crowd, and then it would be time.

"You mustn't do this," Ralf said to her.

"I'm doing it," Estrild replied.

"The druids and the Council all know," he said. "*They're ready for you.*"

She turned her back to him.

The cry went up from the crowd: "New warriors!"

The boys—and Estrild, with them—pounded their spears in unison on the ground and began to move forward.

In her thirteen years of life, Estrild had never felt such exhilaration. It was as if everything came together in that moment: the spring weather, which she had always loved; the sight of a solitary hawk that in that moment soared with outstretched wings in an arc across the blue sky; the brief shake of the earth she could feel beneath her feet as the blunt ends of the spears pounded there; the collective gasp of admiration she could hear from the onlookers as the group emerged from the woods and moved, stomping and chanting, across the clearing; the low roars and wuffs echoing against the shields as they performed the *barritas* of war chants; and mostly . . .

. . . *mostly that the time had come. For her. For her sisters and her friends and the future for all women.*

It did not take long for the group to cross the short distance that brought them to the central space where now they stopped abruptly and stood before the Council, which was surrounded by the semicircle of robed druids. They lowered their shields slightly, held their spears erect, and waited.

The crowd had fallen silent now and was watching. Estrild wasn't able to look for her mother or her friends; the females were grouped at the back of the clearing and she couldn't see them from where she was. But from her place at the end of the first line, Estrild found, in the gathered audience of men, her friend Varick standing at the edge. His eyes were on her. She gave a very slight nod of her head and he nodded in return. She noticed with affection that his unruly hair was tied back with the strip of cloth that she had given him.

"THE GIRL ESTRILD!"

What? She blinked. Had she really heard her name announced by the chief druid? *Why was she called first?*

With his elbow, Ralf nudged her roughly. Confused, Estrild turned toward him with a questioning look. What was she supposed to do?

"Move forward," Ralf said under his breath. He reached his hand to her back and shoved. She stumbled ahead one step and stood there alone.

Then she heard the crowd of villagers begin to whisper to one another. Only now were most of them becoming aware that one of the new warriors was, amazingly, a girl. Estrild. There were murmurs. Nervous laughter. Expressions of shock.

She willed herself to stand straighter, to hold her shield higher. Her chin went up. She planted her feet, first one, then the other, on the ground with firm stamps. Then she waited.

And she could see that what Ralf had told her was true: the Council and the druids had known. They were unsurprised.

She could sense this, as well: They were hostile.

Suddenly she was afraid. Her legs, the same strong legs that had crouched and stamped with such vigor on those practice mornings, began to tremble.

The crowd noise subsided as the chief druid motioned with his hand for silence.

"In this tribe," he said, speaking not to Estrild alone, though his eyes were on her as she stood trembling before him, but to the entire assemblage, "women are revered. In our marriage rites she is reminded that she is to be a partner to a man. She will share his dwelling and bear his children."

He looked out at the crowd and they murmured their assent.

Estrild was trying to prepare the words she would use to explain herself, to exhibit her pride. But she was so frightened, it was hard to think clearly.

"She will be virtuous in all things—" the druid said.

Without thinking, she interrupted him and echoed his words. "I *am* virtuous in all things," she said aloud.

He ignored her and went on: "—or her punishment will be harsh."

He paused. The crowd fell silent.

"An unchaste woman will be flogged," he continued.

Flogged? Estrild felt her knees weaken. But *why?*

"I am not unchaste," she protested, and realized that her voice was timid and muffled by the shield. She lowered the heavy piece of iron. "I am not unchaste!" she repeated in a more forceful tone.

But again he ignored her.

"I am claiming—" she began.

"The girl has no claims," a Councilor declared loudly. "She has no rights to claim." Estrild could hear the crowd's concurrence. *No rights. No claims.* They were all saying it, all repeating it. It angered her.

"I *do* have rights!" she tried to say.

But fear had stolen her voice. She took a deep breath and tried again. "We have . . . I mean, *girls* have—"

The Councilor stepped forward. He glanced back to the hooded druid, who nodded. Then the Councilor clamped his hand across her mouth, muffling her voice. "Silence!"

I am powerful, she tried to remind herself.

But with her voice taken, she had lost any feeling of power. She felt weak and hopeless and alone. The druid's words continued but seemed hollow and echoey in her ears; she couldn't understand what he was saying. Her hand, moist with sweat, slipped from the handle of the shield; it fell to the ground and lay useless there.

"The girl Estrild—" She heard that part. Her name.

"—has renounced her womanhood," the druid continued.

"No!" she said, but she was saying it inside her head. "I have *claimed* my—"

He continued. "She has disgraced her body."

She saw him nod to the Councilor, who removed his hand from her mouth and with one quick, sure motion grasped the top of the tunic she was wearing and pulled downward, so that it tore and fell to the ground in a heap beside the shield. Now she stood naked, shocked and terrified. A druid came forward and with one hand grabbed the Suebian knot that she had proudly created that morning. He held a sharp tool in his other hand and used it to scrape and tear at her head; within seconds a mound of her own blond hair, its intricate knot still perfectly formed, lay by her feet.

The crowd, watching, was silent.

"The Council will pronounce the sentence." The druid and the Councilor who had held her both stepped backwards and resumed their place in the semicircle of judgment. Her vision was blurred now, and she felt faint. But she saw that one of the Councilors had come forward to address the watching populace.

"She will be taken and drowned in the bog," he said loudly.

Estrild heard, suddenly, an anguished moan that she knew came from her mother.

"Blindfold her!" A high voice called, and even in her state of combined panic and bewilderment, she realized that someone, some woman, intended it as a kind of comfort, that she should not be forced to look upon the horrors they were about to inflict.

Then, suddenly, she was aware that a person had come from the crowd, had run forward and was handing something to the Councilor. "Here," the person said. She saw that it was Varick, his tangled hair now haloed around his head; he had pulled away the strip of woven cloth and offered it to become her blindfold. The Councilor's hands were rough as he tied it now around her head. But she welcomed it, was grateful for the final gift of darkness, as they reached for her, to grasp her arms and lead her to the bog.

The villagers, watching, had fallen into a shocked silence. But as they led her, stumbling, away, she could hear something. Just a murmur, at first: hushed and tentative. It was a whispered chorus made up of the voices of women and girls. They were asking questions of each other: questions about the future. The soft sound of it cushioned her with hope for them all.

PART THREE

HISTORY

I confess. It was excruciating for me to write the final paragraphs of Estrild's story. Yet it had been clear, from the beginning, from the body found in the bog, how the story would end for her.

I found it intriguing, and I enjoyed going to the old documents, to the photographs, to read the theories and then to put my own imagination to work on the puzzle of the first-century girl. We all know what to do with puzzles, of course—during the recent pandemic a lot of us found our dining room tables covered with jigsaw pieces. It's just a matter of finding the bits of color, the hints and clues that allow us to put the pieces together. And that's what I did.

But once I did that—connected the pieces and imagined her story—Estrild became real to me. I admired her ambition and smiled at her stubbornness. She had a remarkable grit, much more than I had had at thirteen. When the time came for her to die, I had to look away. I didn't accompany her into the bog. It made me too sad.

Could this imagined story have been, in fact, the real story of the Windeby Girl? My guess is no. Although we admire tales of early feminism and strong young woman (Joan of Arc from the fifteenth century has even become a saint!), the rules for females in that very early history, the first century, the Iron Age, were probably never challenged. Women had a role: a hard one, that of having many babies, burying most of them, nourishing the ones that survived, making their garments and their food, teaching their daughters the necessary skills, and feeding the husbands and growing boys who would go off to hunt the meat and protect the villages and fight the tribal enemies. They probably complained now and then. But there wouldn't have been time or energy or any encouragement for even the gentlest rebellion. So Estrild's story is a made-up one. It is fiction. I hope you rooted for her anyway.

But that isn't the end. Along the way I discovered a new and important puzzle piece, something that would reshape the narrative.

The true story of the bog body that had been known as the Windeby Girl changed quite dramatically in the early twenty-first century when a professor of anthropology at the University of North Dakota, Dr. Heather Gill-Robinson, was given a grant to study some of the peat bog mummies in Germany. It had been fifty years since the Windeby Girl had been unearthed. Now new tools—DNA studies, CT scans, 3D imaging—were available to scientists.

Eventually, as a result of her research, Dr. Gill-Robinson reported that in fact the body discovered at Windeby was a boy. She theorized that he was approximately sixteen years old, in poor health, suffering from malnutrition, and likely had died of natural causes. His long blond hair had not been shaved, but probably had been wrenched from his head by the peat-cutting equipment that had uncovered him. And the blindfold? It was no doubt simply a piece of woven cloth that he had used to tie back his hair. At some point it had slipped forward over his forehead.

The story, then, was completely changed.

I was glad, for Estrild's sake.

But what of the boy?

The Iron Age village would remain the same, its small population busy from dawn to dusk with the endless chores that made their harsh lives possible. They would still battle the weather, the hardships, the disease, and the other tribes with whom they had fought for centuries. They would worship and fear and placate the same gods. So now I would revisit that place, searching for the other, truer story. I would create, in my imagination, a sickly, vulnerable teenage boy.

No, wait! I had already created him! I realized

that the boy was there on the pages I had written, the story that I was about to discard. I would start again. This time, I decided, I would focus on Varick, the orphaned, half-starved teenager who loved nature and longed for a family.

PART FOUR

VARICK'S STORY

ONE BRAVE
GOOD THING

He found the little skeleton at the edge of the meadow. The whiteness of the tiny bones glistened in the summer afternoon sunlight and had caught his eye. Crouching there, he carefully brushed away the remaining tufts of feathers and grasses. Then he examined it, how it was put together, and wondered what the best way would be to pick the tiny structure up. It was so fragile.

"Varick?" A shadow fell across the sunny spot where his hands were cupped around the skeleton. He cringed, startled by the voice, and leaned forward in hopes of hiding what he held. The village boys, he knew, would shove him to the side, stomp and crush his little treasure in an instant, and if he protested would taunt him mercilessly.

He looked up, then relaxed when he saw it was the girl named Estrild. She was the leather-maker's daughter. He knew her, liked her curiosity. "Look," he said, and lifted his hands away.

Her long blond hair lifted in the breeze as she leaned down to see. "Oh! A bird! Poor thing! What happened? Do you think an owl got it?"

"No. An owl would crunch the whole thing up and feed its young with it. I think it probably was sick, and just came here to lie down quietly in the grass and die."

The girl was silent for a moment. Then she said, "My mother told me something once, after my uncle died and I was feeling terribly sad."

"What did she tell you?"

"That it is not time to die until you have done one brave, good thing. My uncle had done that, they told her: had helped his friend on the battlefield.

After that, you are ready and people should not be sad because they will always remember you and your one brave, good thing."

They both looked down at the skeleton of the little bird.

Varick suggested, "Maybe it fought against a hawk trying to get at its young. That would be brave, and good."

"Yes," Estrild agreed, and then speculated further: "And then maybe it was badly injured and came here to die in the grass."

Varick nodded. "It could have happened that way. It would be cooler here in the shade of the grass, and it would be like going to sleep. It probably closed its eyes and had nice dreams about flying."

"I hope so." She leaned forward to look more closely at the small skeleton.

"It's been here quite a while, though, for all the skin and soft parts to disappear."

"Can you tell what kind of bird it was?" She knelt beside him.

"Finch. See the beak?" He pointed.

"Yes."

"You've heard them here in the meadow." He was silent for a moment, then imitated, in the back of his throat, the sound of the finch's song: an interrupted chirping, spritely and musical.

"Yes!" she said, in delight. "I have!"

"And look here." Gently, his finger traced, from the base of the skull, the tiny chain of miniature bones attached to one another. "You know how a bird leans its head down and cleans its own feathers, even pecks under its own wings?"

Estrild nodded.

"You and I wouldn't be able to do that." Briefly, he tilted his head forward as if he were a bird and lifted his arm to try to groom himself as a bird might. But he couldn't reach. "He could, because of all these little neck bones. We don't have that many."

"He?"

Varick laughed. "Or she. I can't tell."

Estrild stood and picked up the cloth bag she had set on the path. "I must go," she said. "I'm to take lunch to my brothers. They'll be wondering where

I am." She raised her hand to her forehead to shade her eyes and looked toward the far field. In the distance, he could see her older brothers at work there. Varick knew them; Alard was just his age, Carolus slightly older. Both had already been named warriors, and celebrated. Next battle, they'd be off to it, and the girls, Estrild and her sisters—and their mother, too—would join their father, the leather-maker, and take over caring for the field and the crops. But for now the boys were there, at work.

"Would you like this?" he asked her, gesturing toward the skeleton as she prepared to leave.

"Oh, I don't think so. What would—" Then she hesitated. "Yes," she said.

"I'll bring it to you later," he told her.

"Thank you." Then she added, with a grin, "Chirp!"

"Chirp chirp!" Varck replied, laughing.

It was a back-and-forth that they had enjoyed for several years. A little code; a joke. Varick was still chuckling as she walked away toward the far field. Then he untied the cloth he wore knotted around his neck, laid it on the ground, and began with infinite care to lift the skeleton onto the square of fabric. Like a shroud, he thought, as he folded the corners over the little finch's remains.

Varick had seen many shrouds in his sixteen years of life. He didn't remember his mother, who had died at his birth. But he had a vague memory of watching them wrap his father's body, years ago when he was still a small boy.

Had his father done one brave, good thing before he died? he wondered now. And he decided: *Yes. He had looked at the crookedly built baby that had killed his wife and gave it a name and told them to let it live.*

Carefully he placed the packaged bird in his carrying pouch. He rose to his knees from the place where he had crouched and then stood, awkwardly. Then, with the lurching gait caused by his misshapen spine, he headed back to the shed where he lived, and to the grueling work that was assigned to him every day by his master.

✷

He was not a slave, though there were slaves in the village. And he was not an apprentice, though there were those as well. He was simply a boy who had had bad luck. He had been born flawed to a woman who had died in the birthing. Cared for by neighboring women who barely noticed one more mouth added to the broods they were already feeding, he was kept alive, nothing more. He had never been hugged or tickled or soothed.

His father had named him and paid for his milk and bread but rarely set eyes upon him. A warrior of some rank, he had returned now and then to the village, remembered he had a son and settled some coins for his keep, reminded sadly each time of the twisted spine that meant his boy would never ride a horse or aim a spear.

And then his father, too, was gone: a long march, a brutal battle against a larger tribe, a distant hillside drenched in blood and bodies carried home to be washed and mourned and buried. His shield and spear would have been given to his son, had his son been deemed worthy. But no one thought the boy anything other than useless, with no more worth than a stray dog. His father's weapons were taken to the smelting furnace and the iron from them was given to the forger, who agreed in return to let the boy sleep in a nearby shed and work for his keep. Varick had been five years old.

The work was hard and unrewarding. When the forger ordered it, Varick pushed rhythmically on the leather bellows, which fed breath to the fire and kept the flames leaping and so hot that the air above shimmered and distorted the objects beyond. Sometimes his hair was singed. His arms were dotted with burns from sparks that spit themselves out of the fire, and one knee was branded because he had knelt without noticing the half-shaped nail that had fallen from the anvil and lay there still white-hot on the earth.

Sometimes he fell asleep pushing the bellows and the forger would kick him awake.

He forgot his father's name but remembered his own, though no one called him by it. The iron forger summoned him by shouting: *Boy!*

He was always hungry.

Winters were hardest, for there was no door to the shed where he slept, and the bitter wind found its way in. He slept on straw and welcomed the rats that made their homes in it because he could pretend that their fur was warm. He was glad when it snowed because he could plaster snow across the open gaps in the walls of the shed and build a barrier in front of the door opening, with just enough room to squeeze himself in and out, so that the air inside warmed slightly from the steam of his exhaled breath. Once a large dog, seeking warmth, wandered in and stayed the night; it curled beside Varick and he stroked it and fed it some saved scraps of bread; it returned after that, most nights, and its presence cheered and warmed him. He gave the dog a name. He called it Friend. In the spring it stopped coming and he understood that it had returned to its tasks, herding sheep perhaps, or pulling a heavy cart to the marketplace.

But when spring came, he was happy. The work was no less punishing, but in the times when there was a break in the day, when his work was finished or the forger had to go elsewhere for a task, Varick ran down the path to the meadow and the woods beyond. He could breathe, there.

The other children had always scorned him, had turned their backs when he tried to join their games. They cruelly mimicked his awkward walk and taunted him when he ventured out into the village. But the meadow and the woods were welcoming. At first they seemed quiet. Then, as he learned to listen, he discovered a world of voices. He heard the soft bleat of newborn lambs romping near their mothers, the chirr and flutter of insects in the high grasses, and the impatient squawk of nestlings demanding to be fed.

He began, especially, to know the birds. The steady *sirrrrr* of the waxwings who nested at the edge of the pine forest meant that both the father, with his shaggy crest, pink-tinged face, and flamboyantly red-tipped wings, and his less colorful mate were gathering flying insects for their hungry brood.

The loud *ooo-hu, ooo-hu* at twilight told him that the huge orange-eyed owl who lived at the edge of the bog would be soaring low across the fields to plunge its talons into the neck of the hare it had spotted. The owl lived close to the ground, nested in an outcropping of moss-coated rocks. Sometimes he saw it sit motionless and watching, perched on the tree-branch fence that enclosed a small group of goats, ignoring the noisy scuffling goats but vigilant to the fields and the pond. Varick would see nothing. But the orange eyes would perceive a fish or a weasel, swoop to grab it in an instant and carry it back to its nest, its mate, and their young.

And so the boy found friends. Some of them, rabbits and mice and even some of the birds, came to his outstretched hand. He learned the calls of the orange-eyed owl and eventually, one day when he was twelve years old, he called to it and to his amaze-ment it answered him with a friendly *ooo-hu, wuh wuh wuh.* Making his way that afternoon back to the shed, to the fire, the bellows, the slaps and the scoldings, Varick was smiling.

He took the fragile finch skeleton from his carrying sack and placed it on the shelf that he had built in his sleeping shed. He would take it to Estrild as he had promised. But for now he set it beside the row of other relics he had collected.

His newest and largest treasure was the skull of a calf that had not survived its birth. The farmer, angry that his cow had been unsuccessful in increasing his herd, had left the body to rot in the field. Varick had watched predators, birds and insects and small rodents, peck at and chew away the flesh and entrails until finally there was only the skeleton left. He went there whenever he had the time, to study it, to examine how its bones connected to one another, and to compare them to his own bony formation. Then when he felt he could not teach himself any more from it in the field, he carefully lifted the sun-bleached skull away from the spinal structure and took it back to what he had begun to call, to himself, his Learning Shelf, where it joined the remains of other creatures.

He was hungry for learning—especially to learn the mysteries of his own body. He examined the remains of the calf, closed his eyes and felt how the bones were joined, then pressed on his own skin and felt the contours of his own structure, imagining how everything attached together: different from a calf, but in some ways the same. He went to the field and touched the living cow, felt how her thick sides heaved in and out as she breathed, then considered his own chest and how it moved. Why, he wondered, did animals and people need to pull air into their bodies? He touched her quivering nostrils and smelled her warm, moist breath. He examined her ears and then his own, and their eyes as well, until she pushed his hand aside impatiently with her head and moved away from him.

He caught fish and brought some of them to the forger to be eaten. But others he cut apart very carefully so that he could see the inner parts, and by the time his examination was done there was little left and he threw the remains back into the pond, wiped the sticky scales from his hands, and found himself wondering about skin and all the forms it took. Why did he have pale skin, goose-bumped in winter, instead of a leathery hide? Or fur? He had never seen a bear but knew of them, had heard the descriptions of their thick fur. A man in the village had a cloak made of it.

Varick pondered all of those things and found himself looking carefully at the villagers: how a woman bulged bigger and bigger until she gave birth, in the same way a sheep did; yet the lamb, when it was a healthy one, stood and walked that same day, while a woman's infant was weak and useless, carried about and tended for a year or so. And even then it tottered about stupidly and had to be rescued and set upright again and again if it fell, even as the lamb pranced and played. (Did it know it would be slaughtered? He wondered about that, too.)

No one knew of his Learning Shelf. He had no friends. Boys his age ignored him, now that they had outgrown the small tortures they had inflicted on him when they all were younger. Children like Estrild, to whom he explained what he knew of the natural world, and to whom he sometimes told fanciful stories, were fond of him and felt sorry for him. But they did not love him. No one did.

Except, perhaps, he thought (although he laughed at the thought), the orange-eyed owl. He had never been physically close to the owl, had never reached out his hand to touch it. But it watched him, always, rotating its head his way, sliding a sidelong glance at him as if to catch him at some mischief. He imitated it, turning his own head, staring back, almost playing a game of who-will-look-away-first. And, of course, they talked to each other. It had been several years now since the owl had first murmured a throaty reply to Varick. He had become accustomed to it and no longer found himself wondering, "Did it really—?" It did. He knew that it did.

One early evening in late summer, he returned the finch's skeleton to Estrild. He needed room on his shelf for a dried snakeskin, shimmering with iridescent greens and blue, that he had found at the edge of the pond. She had forgotten about the finch, but her eyes lit up with delight when she saw the little treasure in his hands. "Oh!" she said. "Thank you! I'll make it into a clasp for my shawl!" Then she said, "Wait!" when he turned to leave. She went back inside her dwelling and after a moment returned with a gift for him.

He had never had a gift before. But she handed it to him: a strip of woven cloth. "From my mother's loom," she explained.

Varick touched the soft wool and marveled at its colors, how the brown and yellow and red crossed each other in an intricate pattern. Then, while the girl watched, he used it to tie back his thick mane of tangled hair. He nodded awkwardly as a thank you, and she replied with a smile and her usual "Chirp."

"Chirp chirp!" he said in return, laughing, and continued on his walk.

The sun was very low in the sky, and in the twilight, he strolled past the meadows and the pond, beyond the edges of the forest to where the peat bog lay. People avoided the bog, except for necessary excursions when they would cut peat to be dried and used for fires. The smell was unpleasant, and the thick mud sucked at one's feet. There were biting insects, and at night, often, flashing glimmers of light that some people said were evil spirits trying to lure one further in, to the darker interior parts. Varick didn't believe that. He thought the lights were simply tiny flickers of lightning, somehow created by the murky air and moisture, as lightning was.

And despite the odor, the bog fascinated him. It

was a place of secrets, unlike the open meadow where things flew and leaped and sang. The bog was dank and silent and seemed to whisper; sometimes he felt that it was inviting him in.

Today he was surprised to find someone else on the bog path. He had seen the old man before, in the village. It was rare for people to live to a great age, so he had noticed this man, whose body was bent over and whose white beard and long hair were thin. When he smiled a greeting, Varick could see that he had few teeth. But his eyes seemed keen and alert.

"Good evening," the man said.

"Hello," Varick replied.

"Out for a stroll? Would you like company?" the man asked.

Varick wouldn't; he preferred to be alone. But he didn't want to be unkind. So he smiled and nodded. They walked side by side silently for a bit. Varick's walk, because of his twisted spine, was always slow, and the old man shuffled, his leather sandals scraping at the stony path.

"I often come out here in the early evening," the

man told him. "There's a rock up ahead, where I sit and watch the birds."

"I know that rock," Varick said. "You can see the pond from there."

"Listen!" the man said.

They paused on the path and Varick heard the irritable squawks of waterfowl. "Settling in for the night. Fighting over their favorite spots," the old man said. Then he suddenly held up one hand. "Shhh!" he said. "Here he comes!"

It was a familiar sound to Varick: the slow, heavy wing-flap. He turned and saw first the shadow moving across the grass, then the orange-eyed owl itself, flying low as it returned to its home in the rocks at the edge of the bog.

"I know him!" Varick said.

His companion chuckled. "I've known him since before you were born," he said. "He's a very old fellow."

They continued on to the large rock and the man leaned against it, resting. "I study birds," Varick confided.

"They have much to teach us."

"Yes, a bird's neck has more bones than—"

"A bird takes care of its young. That owl? He and his mate have raised families year after year. They have young in the nest right now. That's why he spends so much time hunting for food."

"Yes. I like to examine the—"

But the old man wasn't listening. "He's slowing down, though. I think he's coming to the end of his days. As I am."

Varick was startled. He had never thought before about birds growing old. But nothing more was said. The two stayed there together for a while, silently, leaning against the boulder, as the sun set behind the line of distant trees.

The days of summer passed. By the end of the crop-growing season Varick had stopped visiting the headless remains of the calf. He thought he had learned all he could from it, though he still studied its skull on his shelf, imagining what had been inside, in the mysterious hollow surrounded by bone.

Varick and the old man met from time to time at the large rock and watched night fall over the pond and fields. In midsummer the light had remained until late evening, but now the sky darkened earlier. Some of the waterfowl had gathered in flocks and flown away to whatever unknown place kept them warm in the winter months. The pine trees in the forest remained thick and dark green, but other trees began to change; their leaves were yellow now, and dry. The wind swept through and rustled them into a swoosh of rattling sound, then tore them loose and they swirled across the path. Varick had been barefoot since spring. Now he wore foot coverings that he had made himself of wood and scraps of animal hide. The orange-eyed owl still swooped past them as it headed toward its kill: a fish in the pond, a rabbit in the tall grass. It returned with dinner dangling from its talons, but its nest was empty now of young.

The owl seemed slower, and tired. Mostly it ignored the humans who watched it, though occasionally from the fence post where it sometimes rested, it still swiveled its neck to stare at Varick.

Sometimes it uttered its mournful *ooo-hu, ooo-hu,* and Varick replied.

"He has no enemies, does he?" Varick asked his elderly friend one evening, speaking of the owl after it had made its evening foray and swooped past them, heading home. "Because he's so *big.*"

The old man chuckled. "He *looks* big," he replied. "But underneath all those feathers, his body is actually quite small. You'd be surprised."

Varick imagined the skeleton of the owl, surprisingly small, on his Learning Shelf. It would be a treasure. But it would mean that the owl's life had ended.

"How will he die?" he asked.

The man shrugged his hunched, thin shoulders. "If he lives through the winter, he may go out one morning in the spring to find food and be too weak to return. He's spent many years feeding his young, and he's tired now. He may settle to rest in the grass of a field and be trampled by the oxen as they plow.

"But I don't think he will last the winter. I think the day will come, one day soon, when his energy is gone. He'll know. He'll find a place of comfort and he'll huddle with his wings folded, and he'll go to sleep and not wake."

Varick accepted that. It seemed right.

"I'll do the same," the old man said with a chuckle.

"We all will, someday," Varick announced in a loud voice. It seemed less frightening that way, if they stopped talking softly. "Even the bad-tempered woman who's always shoving people when they're lined up at the well. You know the one I mean? She won't last forever."

The old man nodded and laughed aloud. "I do indeed. And what about that very arrogant boy named Ralf?"

"Yes, Ralf! He bloodied my nose once! And—" Varick hesitated. His thought was sacrilegious, he knew. But he said it anyway. "The druids! Them, too!"

"Wearing their gold collars and their hoods?" the man asked. Now they were both laughing. The thought of the owl's death—and their own, and everyone's—became something lighthearted, something far distant, when they laughed at it.

They both shivered in the wind as the sun dropped behind the trees.

The iron-forger fell, early one morning in autumn. He blamed Varick, though they both knew there was no blame. Varick had not left tools on the ground for the forger to stumble over, or spilled oil. But it had turned quite cold suddenly overnight, and in the early morning there was a thin coat of frost on the hard dirt floor of the iron forge. Beyond the overhang of the thatched roof, icy needles of sleet were falling. The man had risen and emerged from his hut unaware of the change in the weather. His feet had slipped on the unexpected ice and he fell hard on the frozen ground. Then he looked for someone to shout at in anger.

"Boy!"

Varick, just emerging from the shed where he slept, hoping for breakfast, hurried to kneel beside the forger where he lay groaning on the ground.

"You fool! I told you always to sweep everything up! Now look what's happened!" The forger grabbed at his right leg, tried to bend it, but gave a harsh cry of pain and fell back.

Varick reached for a folded leather apron that was nearby and pulled it over to cushion the man's head. He listened to the man's muffled groaning and noticed how his leg lay at an odd angle. He thought about what to do. He remembered how, in the nights when the dog lay beside him, he had run his hand along its legs, feeling the structure of them, comparing it with his own.

"Will you let me try to help you?" he asked the forger.

The man panted, tried to move, and cursed. "How could an imbecile like you help me?" he asked hoarsely.

"I could get you some willow bark from the shed. I chew it to ease the pain in my back. It helps."

"Get me some, then."

Varick hurried to the place where he kept the bark and brought some to the man. It was true that the medicine of the willow eased the dull, everyday ache caused by his misshapen spine. He had no idea if it would help his injured master. But he gave him a piece to chew.

Then he said, "May I feel your leg?"

"What do you know of legs?"

"I learned from the skeleton of a calf. And then I felt a dog's body carefully. They're built differently, of course, but I learned how the parts attach to each other."

"You're a damned fool. Bring me cider."

"Yes. That will help." Varick rose and went into the man's dwelling hut to find the large jug of cider. The fermented apple drink certainly made the men of the village feel happy, though sometimes the happiness turned to a wild sort of madness, and usually ended with broken furniture, puke-stained clothing, and a snoring stupor. He brought a tankard of the cider, knelt again, put his arm around the forger's shoulder, and lifted his head to help him drink. "Now may I feel your leg?" he asked.

"Another!"

Varick helped him drink again, several large gulps, and then eased his head back to the folded apron. The forger grunted, closed his eyes, and chewed on the piece of bark.

He moved his hands down cautiously to the man's right leg. He knew from his study of the dead calf that there were three big bones in the leg: one from the foot to a kind of joint like an elbow, then another from that to a sort of knee, and then one bigger bone from the knee up to the main body of the animal. A dog was different, more like a person, with just two main leg parts with one jointed place in the middle, but a dog's ankle and foot were very complicated. He wished that he had found a way to study the skeleton of a man. He had carefully pressed on his own leg many times, to feel its structure, and thought he knew that a man had perhaps two bones below the knee, and one long, larger bone above.

When he reached down to the upper right of the forger's limb, he expected to feel that the one large bone was broken. He had begun to plan how he would secure it if he could fit the broken pieces together. He thought that he could use the iron poker with which the forger stirred his fire as a support for the broken bone if he could manage to maneuver the two parts into place. He wished there were a second poker so that he could secure and immobilize the leg between two firm supports. But without that, he would use a good thick length of wood; there were plenty of those, leaning against the wall. Then he would need strips of cloth to secure everything. When he had gone into the hut to get the cider, he had seen bedding strewn messily over a straw-filled mattress in the corner. He would tear some of the bedding to make the strips he would use.

Then, holding everything in place, he would—

No. He paused and felt more carefully. He realized that he had guessed wrong. The upper leg bone was intact, not broken at all. But something was—

The forger groaned. "More!" he demanded. Varick lifted him again and held the tankard while he gulped the last of the cider, then lay back and took several deep breaths.

Varick set the empty tankard aside and again placed his hands on the leg. Carefully, moving his hands as gently as he could, he felt its length. The problem was at the very top of the leg, where it met the man's hip.

He moved to the other side and felt the left, uninjured leg, again moving his hands from the ankle to the knee, then upward to the top. The difference was clear. At the top of the forger's left leg, the bone fit smoothly into his hip socket. Varick remembered, from the decomposing body of the calf, how the parts fit together and were held in place by strong, moist, stretchable bands. He had watched day by day as those parts, the bands, had dried in the sun and were pecked at by birds. Now he tried to picture beneath the coarse fabric of the iron-forger's trousers, through the thick, hairy layer of his skin and beyond the slick vessels that carried his blood, into the place where his healthy left leg bone curved into a ball at the end and nestled, held tight there, in the place where it could rotate as the man walked and knelt and leaned. At the top of the right leg— Varick's hands now felt there—that rounded end of the bone had come out of its place. He could feel it, under the skin, protruding out of the socket where it should be tightly lodged.

He knew, though he dreaded it, what he must do. He wiped his sweat-glistened hands on his vest. "I'll get you some more cider," he murmured, and went back into the hut to refill the tankard. But when he returned, he felt uneasy. Unready. Scared. If it didn't go well—if he did further damage to the iron-forger's leg—they would judge him. He would likely be put to death.

But the man was suffering. And he thought he could help him. He lifted the forger's head, held the tankard for him, then said, "I'm going to go off for a bit, and you'll be here alone. If you don't try to move, you won't be in pain. Just lie very still until I return."

"Ungrateful brat," the forger mumbled.

"No. I'm not. I'm going to fix your leg. But I need to do one thing first, to make sure I'm doing it right."

"*Make sure?*"

"Yes." Varick wiped spilled cider from the man's beard with a cloth he had brought from the hut. "Lie still."

"You'll come back?" The forger, whimpering, seemed childlike now.

"Yes. I'll hurry."

"I'm cold."

Ordinarily the embers of the forger's fire, the one Varick stoked again and again with the bellows, would be waiting to be stirred and rekindled in the morning. But this morning the ashes were black and cold; wind had blown sleet into the sheltered area during the night and extinguished the fire. It would take some time to reignite it, and Varick realized that he needed this time for a different, more important task. So he ignored the ashes. Instead, he brought a dirty woven blanket from the hut and covered the man where he lay. The sleet was coming fast now, beyond the roof covering, making staccato taps on the icy path, and he was tempted to wrap the blanket around himself. But he could warm himself, he thought, by running, and the man was unable to move. So he tucked the blanket around the shivering shoulders, and said again, "I'll hurry." Then he ran with his lurching gait from the forge toward the field where the calf skeleton still lay.

Ordinarily, at dawn, the villagers rose and went about their outdoor tasks. But today's weather kept them in their dwellings. He saw no one. Smoke came from the chimney holes on the dwelling roofs. Varick ran past a fenced enclosure where two horses stood with their heads down, steamy breath in plumes from their nostrils. And somewhere a dog barked. He wished it were Friend, and that it would come and run beside him. But he was alone. There were no other signs of life.

Fortunately, he knew exactly where to find the calf, though it was deep now in high grass that had grown around it during the summer season. He knelt and pushed the stiff browned grass aside. He found a rear leg and felt its length. He had realized before how different it was from a human leg. Still, the top bone was rounded and fit neatly into the hollow of the hip socket in the same way a man's did. He tugged at that bone. For a moment he thought it would not come loose, but he pulled harder and quite suddenly it popped out and upward. The cords that had held it in place were eaten away and gone, but he envisioned how they would have held firmly to the leg bone even when it was wrenched loose. He could picture in his mind how tightly such cords gripped the forger's bone and how—he did this now, with his hands—he would need to pull *down* on it, and *out*, to position it, and then let it snap back into the place where it should be.

His blew on his hands, and held them briefly in his armpits, to warm them. It was bitter cold. He took deep breaths and felt the icy air slice into him. He leaned forward, his bare knees on the frozen ground, to practice again and again, pulling the calf's long leg bone forward and out, holding it poised at the correct angle, and letting it slip back into its intended place. He tried to memorize that angle, the placement of his hands, the kind of pressure he would need to use when he returned to the place where the forger waited.

Repositioning the bone in the man's leg, he realized, with the stretched bands intact, would take great strength. But his arms were strong, he knew. His back was weakened by the curvature in his spine, and his legs had always struggled. But his arms had made up for those weaknesses. He had lifted heavy pieces of iron, had wrestled the anvil from one location in the forge to another, had carried the buckets of peat and wood. His arm muscles were hardened and firm.

Drenched and shivering now from the splattering sleet, Varick finally took one last deep breath, rose with a sense of determination from the skeleton, and headed back to fix the iron-forger's leg.

No one heard the screams of pain. If they did, perhaps they thought it was the sound of a slave being whipped. It was dawn, with wind howling and sleet clattering on the icy ground, and no one came to see what was wrong.

And it worked. The plan that Varick had made worked.

He had described it first, carefully, to the forger when he returned. The man had not moved; his eyes were closed. But he heard the boy return and he stirred slightly. Varick leaned over and touched his shoulder.

The forger moaned and opened his eyes. "You're back," he said in a hoarse voice.

"Yes. And I've figured out exactly what to do." He lifted the blanket from the man and set it aside.

"To do?"

"There's a long bone at the top of your leg," Varick explained to him. "It's supposed to fit nicely into your hip. But yours—"

"Came loose," the forger muttered. "I felt it come loose. It popped out."

"Yes, that's right. And I need to pop it back into place."

The forger stared at him.

"It's attached by some stretchy parts. But they've pulled out of their place. So I'll have to pull the leg *down* first, and get it into the right position, and then the stretchy cords will help it back into the place where it should be."

The forger groaned. "Get the druids. They'll call on the gods to help."

Varick took a deep breath. "I think the gods— and the druids—want *us* to do this hard part. After that, we'll offer thanks."

"You sure it'll work?" The forger stared at him.

Varick lied. "Yes," he said.

"Go ahead, then. Get me more cider first."

"I will. But first I have to explain how I'm going to do this. My arms are strong enough. I have very strong arms. But—"

"You do have strong arms for such a crooked-backed boy. I've watched you swing the hammer."

The iron-headed hammer that was used to shape

the tools had a thick wooden handle and was immensely heavy. When he was younger, Varick had not been able even to lift it. Now, with effort, he could lift it over his head and swing it down. The forger had allowed him to try doing some shaping of unimportant parts. Varick had made a mess of it, of the shaping; but he had learned to swing the weighty hammer.

"Yes. My arms are strong enough to do this. But I have to place myself in the right position. I have to brace myself against something."

"Where's that cider?" The forger turned his head and looked toward the empty tankard near him still on the ground.

"I'll get it, I promise. But I'm just explaining that when we're ready, after I've given you plenty of cider, I'm going to place my right foot up between your two legs and wedge it there while I get a good grip on your right leg, just above the knee—"

The forger's eyes opened wide. "No," he said.

"I'll be very careful. I'll have to put my foot *here*—" Varick leaned forward and gently placed his hand on the forger's groin.

The iron-forger raised himself and slapped the hand away. Then he sank back down and groaned with pain.

"It should only be for a minute. I just need to have something to push against while I tug your leg down and move it into place."

"NO."

Varick sighed and sat back on his heels. It was clear that he would have to create a new plan. He glanced around and spotted the massive iron anvil beside the cold ashy remnants of the fire. He had moved it before. It was unliftable—much too heavy—but he had shoved it into position occasionally, with difficulty, when the forger had asked him to. He would do so now.

First he brought more cider and helped the man take a few gulps. Then he shoved the anvil an inch, two inches. Next, more cider. He went back and forth several times. Cider. Anvil. Cider again. Another two inches of the anvil across the earth. Then: cider.

Finally he sat back, panting. The anvil was in place. The man, his beard matted and sodden with drink, was snoring.

Varick arranged himself, planted his foot against the anvil for leverage, and grasped the forger's thigh. But he realized, as he was about to summon his arms' strength, that his plan wouldn't work; he would pull the entire body of the man forward. He needed the body to be held in place as he pulled only the bone of the leg. He realized he would have to disobey that shouted NO.

He rearranged himself. He summoned his courage. Silently he raised himself on his left knee, again grasped the forger's thigh, and extended his right leg to wedge his foot in the man's groin. The forger grunted slightly and snored. Varick took two deep breaths to ready himself; then he pulled as hard as he could on the iron-forger's leg.

The forger screamed and waved his arms wildly. Varick kept his grip tight, pulled even harder, and the man screamed again. Suddenly the dislocated bone moved downward and sideways, then slid with a click into place.

The two of them took deep, satisfied breaths which steamed in the frigid air. Both of their foreheads were shiny with sweat.

"Thank you," the iron-forger whispered. "You're a good boy."

They were the first kind words the man had ever spoken to him, but Varick didn't hear. He felt suddenly faint. The world around him blurred, and in a kind of dream he saw the orange-eyed owl swoop past a calf plodding contentedly across a meadow, and behind them were the flickering lights of the nighttime bog. Bright-colored butterflies darted here and there. Then everything swirled together into a dizzying mass of colors; there was a great hollow sound of onrushing wind, and he fell forward into darkness.

When he woke, he was alone, lying on the frozen ground beside the anvil. The sleet outside had softened into snowfall and the world beyond the forge was white. His clothing had stiffened with frost and made cracking sounds as he sat up. The forger was gone but Varick could see from the way the sawdust and iron shavings had been parted and flattened on the ground that the man had dragged himself into his hut. Dizzy, confused, afraid to try to stand, he crawled to the hut's half-open door. His body felt strange, as if it were separate from the rest of himself.

From the doorway he peered through the shadowy interior and saw the man lying on the straw-filled mattress. Loud snores each ended in a liquid whistle occasionally punctuated by a gurgling cough: the same sounds Varick had heard often enough during nights when the forger had been drinking with his friends. So he was alive. He was asleep. And it appeared, from the way that he was sprawled on the mattress with his legs comfortably stretched out, that his right hip had held.

With no sun, and only the whirling snow outside, Varick could not guess the time of day. He could see that on the simple table in the center of the forger's hut there was an apple and a torn loaf of grainy bread. Ordinarily he would have been given a chunk of the bread at daybreak; he had been on his way to that very breakfast when he saw the forger slip and fall. So he had never eaten anything today. But he didn't feel hungry, just lightheaded and terribly tired. He pulled himself up by holding on to the door, returned shakily to the place where the anvil stood, and picked up the blanket that had been left there. No doubt he would be punished for this, perhaps accused of theft. But he didn't care at that moment. He was so wretchedly cold. He wrapped the blanket around himself, over his icy clothing, and stumbled through the snow to the miserable shed where he lived. There, beneath the Learning Shelf, Varick sank onto the pile of straw that was his bed.

At some time during the hours that followed, the dog he had named Friend appeared, sniffed at the doorway, entered the shed, and curled himself beside the semiconscious boy.

Over the course of many days, the iron-forger very gradually recovered from his accident. Although it was part of his nature to grumble loudly about most things, and everyone who stopped in to see him listened to his noisy complaints about the ache in his leg, the disruption of his work, the poor quality of his food, and the biting insects in his straw mattress, he never spoke harshly of the boy. Instead, he talked with a sort of wonder about how Varick had happened on him after he fell and had treated him with courage, kindness, and intelligence.

"He values learning," the forger explained. "That's how he knew what to do. He studies about bones."

"How do you study about bones?" the leather-maker's wife asked, with a frown. She had brought a pot of soup from her dwelling. People came each day with gifts of food because the forger had no wife and could not yet walk. "I made this from a stag's bone. I added onions and herbs. But I didn't *study* it."

"Maybe he wants to be a druid," a neighbor, standing in the doorway, suggested. "They study the bones and innards for portents."

"That's right," the leather-maker's wife agreed. "The druids throw a pile of bones on the altar and then move them around, looking for signs. They can tell the future, the druids, from bones. Or so they say."

The forger waved his hand impatiently. "No, this is different." But he didn't try to explain. He didn't really understand it himself, how the lurching orphan that he had ordered about for years had somehow created a secret life of some sort, how he had learned to value the things he brought home from the fields and the bog and the woods: rocks with moss, dead rodents, feathers, beetles and snakeskins and skulls. And how he used what he had learned from them to put back together the same man who had slapped and ridiculed and starved him for all this time.

The iron-forger felt something he didn't have a name for. It was shame.

"Where's the boy now?" the neighbor asked, looking around. "Lazy brat. He should be tending this fire."

"No. I told him to rest," the forger muttered. "He's poorly. He has a bad cough."

"I'll send my daughter over with some honey," the leather-maker's wife said as she turned to go. "It's good for coughs."

She and the neighbor turned away, talking to each other about this year's bees, how much honey they had made, whether the hives would survive this coming winter if already so early in the fall the weather was so harsh.

"I'll bring you bread later," the neighbor called over her shoulder.

The forger, alone in his hut, leaned on the iron poker and tried standing. Very carefully he allowed a small amount of his weight to rest on the right leg. The pain had lessened. Soon, he thought, he'd be able to walk, and by then the boy would be well. The two of them would resume their regular life. He would send Varick to the marketplace again, for bread and cider. But he would be kinder to him, would speak a little more gently. Maybe he would teach the boy how to shape and hammer the nails and small tools that were his usual winter livelihood.

Probably, he thought, he should have asked the two pesky women to take some food over to the shed where the boy lay sick. He couldn't get there himself, not with the hip still healing. And the last time the boy had stumbled, coughing, over to the forge and sipped some soup had been two days ago. His sickness was lasting too long. It was worrisome. But there was nothing the forger could do, he thought, except wait.

In the shed, Varick lay panting, shivering, gasping for each breath and drenched with sweat on the heap of straw. The dog came and went, off to whoever his master was, to his chores, reappearing occasionally to sleep beside the boy, who did not have the energy to stroke him. Varick no longer thought about the dog. Nor was he thinking of the iron-forger, or of the rats that had gnawed at the hardened crust of bread he had brought back here the last time he had made his way up to the forge for food. He thought of nothing, really, only the searing pain in his chest that surged through him with each cough. The straw around his face was wet and slippery with the thick yellow fluid that he spat there.

The girl—Estrild, was that her name?—had looked in, had brought him a warm drink of something, and had rearranged the blanket over him. She had pointed with a smile to the strip of cloth he still wore to hold back his hair, the woven strip her mother had made. She saw his Learning Shelf, admired the calf's skull, and reminded him of the little finch bones he had given her. She was going to make something with them; he couldn't remember what, exactly.

"Chirp!" she said to him, and smoothed his hair.

He was supposed to say something back, he knew. But he had no energy for it.

And the old man! Yes! He had come, too. He too had admired the shelf, had spoken of the things they would find, the things they could learn from, when spring came and the weather was warm again. The old man and the girl had both spoken of the frigid weather, the ice outside, and the wind.

. But surprisingly, Varick didn't feel cold. From time to time he did shake with chills, but then the shaking would subside and warmth enveloped him. It felt like an afternoon in summer, as if the sun beat down. He shoved the blanket aside and pulled open his vest. He began to think that perhaps he could go outside so that the cold air, the wind they had described, might cool him. But when he tried to stand, a cough bent him double. It was hard to catch his breath, and his legs trembled, so he lay back on the straw and drifted to sleep again. He dreamed of the orange-eyed owl.

In the night, he woke again and vaguely remembered the dream. It was as if the owl were there beside him in the shed. He could almost hear the heavy flap of the vast feathered wings. He drifted in and out of sleep, in and out of the owl dream. He had never felt so hot. He yearned for the huge wings to rise and fall, to fan and cool him. Finally, again, he tried to stand, and this time his frail legs held him. He found his way to the door of the shed, felt the frosty ground with his bare foot, then went out of doors and stood on the icy path. There was a moon.

He staggered along the path, past the silent dwellings of the sleeping village. A shadow hovered and swooped across the white ground ahead of him. Wings? Perhaps.

Ooo-huh, ooo-huh.

"It's me! It's Varick! I'm coming," he replied.

He moved forward. But it was not like his past days, when despite his lurching gait he still ran with boyish vigor, happy to be in the meadow, at the big rock, to be surrounded by the land, the sounds of the trees, the cry of the birds. Now his vitality was gone. He remembered, suddenly, what the old man had told him of the owl.

He'll know. He'll find a place of comfort and he'll huddle with his wings folded, and he'll go to sleep and not wake.

Varick knew. He continued through the moonlit night, toward the bog, where he would slide his twisted, fever-ridden body into the murky water and he would at last be cool. The orange-eyed owl would be there with him. Above them, the mysterious bog fire would dance with welcoming light. They would not go to sleep. No! Together they would rise though the lights and slide into the air. They would soar.

PART FIVE

HISTORY

Today, in northern Germany, a huge owl with orange eyes and a wingspan of over six feet makes its nest in rocky areas near the edges of forests. They call it the European eagle-owl.

Would the eagle-owl have existed there two thousand years ago? There is simply no way to know for certain. But I decided, in writing Varick's story, that it would.

What I did know for certain at the start of each story was that the Windeby Child—first as Estrild, then as Varick—would die. Yet when that time came, for each of them, I felt ineffably sad. A part of me wanted to rewrite history, to change the endings.

(*Ta-DA! The village took a vote and overruled the decision of the elders and druids, and Estrild went on to an illustrious adulthood, and . . . Or: Yay! Varick's fever broke in the night and when he woke up the next morning he felt much better, and . . .*) But I didn't, of course. Although I was creating fiction, it was to be based on truth. And in truth, a child died. One part of why I wrote the stories was to solve that puzzle, to try to guess at a cause, some reason that meshed with history, for a young person's life to end so abruptly and in such a desolate, forbidding place.

We'll never know, of course, the true reason. I had to guess at possibilities. The Roman historian Tacitus had told us that a person in that place, at that time, would be put to death—specifically, *drowned in the bog*—for "disgracing one's body." And so poor Estrild, innocent of any crime beyond wanting to better the lives of herself, her sisters, and the girls who would follow her, is accused of that crime and sentenced to that fate.

As for Varick? Today's society would find a place

for a boy like him, would see beyond his limitations to his warm heart and keen mind. But not back then. He was born at the wrong time, in the wrong place, and his fate was sealed from the start. He kept himself going, ironically, by chewing on willow bark, a common remedy for pain and inflammation in that time. The Greek physician Hippocrates had written about it three hundred years before Varick was born. But it wasn't discovered until centuries later that willow bark contained acetylsalicylic acid; we know it today as aspirin. Varick's luck ran out when he got pneumonia two thousand years before penicillin. His manner of death would have been a very common one not only in his day but for centuries to come. My own father, born in 1905, had a brother who died of pneumonia as a child.

The two fictional characters I created, Estrild and Varick, were really ahead of their time, out of sync with their century. If we were to pluck Estrild out of the Iron Age and set her down in, say, 1917, she'd very likely cut her hair short and be out there marching with a sign, maybe picketing the White

House on behalf of women's right to vote. There were many women in history, real ones, not made up by an author, who fought for such things. One was the former slave named Sojourner Truth, who in 1851, at the Women's Convention in Ohio, made a speech in which she said, "I have as much muscle as any man, and can do as much work as any man. I have plowed and reaped and husked and chopped and mowed, and can any man do more than that?" I can hear Estrild's voice in her. "*Girls* have rights!" Estrild insisted. She was silenced. But women everywhere speak for her today.

And Varick? He was a budding scientist in the days before science really existed. Ptolemy, the mathematician and astronomer, lived in Egypt in the second century—not long after Varick—but Copernicus and Galileo and DaVinci? The world had to wait hundreds of years, until the fifteenth and sixteenth centuries, for them. Yet there must always have been young people like Varick, curious and studious, and they would have paved the way, even as they remained unknown. Every child who has treasured a collection of seashells, or who has knelt in the garden to examine the workings of a worm—I'll include my own children and grandkids here—has grown out of many centuries of Varicks.

In the stories, putting the puzzle together, I used actual details gleaned from history books: the Suebian knot, for example, that Estrild arranged in her long hair can be found on the skulls of actual Germanic warriors. I looked at photographs of those. The fragment of cloth woven of brown and yellow and red more than two thousand years ago really exists.

And you can visit the Windeby Child. The bog body is housed in a museum in Schleswig-Holstein, Germany, and you can see its face, with its closed eyes and its mouth in what seems, to me, to be a puzzled expression, as if it were asking, *Why?*

Isn't it interesting that the word *history* can be wrenched apart to become "his story"? (*Or hers?*) That's exactly what history consists of: people, and their stories. What happened to them. What caused those things to happen. How they reacted to what happened. How others reacted. And how did they feel on that day, or the day before, or the day before that?

There would have been many Iron Age people living in that village at the edge of the bog. I could have selected any one of them: a druid, perhaps; or Gudrun, the student of midwifery; maybe Ralf, the bully; or the unnamed old man. Each of them had a story of his or her own. So did each person in the next village, the next tribe, the next century, the next country to the north or west. So many stories! Hundreds of them . . . thousands . . . millions . . . billions. They intertwine, connect here and there, until they create the huge, sprawling mass of human existence and what we call history.

Your story is part of that. So is mine.

There is a saying that when people die, they continue to live as long as someone remembers them. I would add: "and tells their story."

That's the other part of what I have tried to do: to tell the story and thereby to let the Windeby Child live.

PHOTO CREDITS

BIBLIOGRAPHY

Aldhouse-Green, Miranda. *Bog Bodies Uncovered.* London: Thames & Hudson Ltd., 2015.

Deem, James M. *Bodies from the Bog.* Boston: Houghton Mifflin Harcourt, 1998.

Glob, P. V. *The Bog People.* New York: New York Review Books, 1965.

Price, T. Douglas. *Europe Before Rome.* New York: Oxford University Press, 2013.

Tacitus. *Agricola Germania.* Revised by J. B. Rives. Translated by Harold Mattingly. London: Penguin Books Ltd., 2009.

THE WANDSWORTH SHIELD BOSS

This image shows a bronze "shield boss"—the central piece of a shield meant to deflect blows to the middle of circular shields and provide a location for a grip to be mounted. Originally found in the River Thames at Wandsworth around 1849, the boss is thought to have been created during the Iron Age, circa the second century BC. The shield features a Celtic style of decoration known as "La Tène," comprised of an intricate pattern of two birds with stylized outstretched wings.

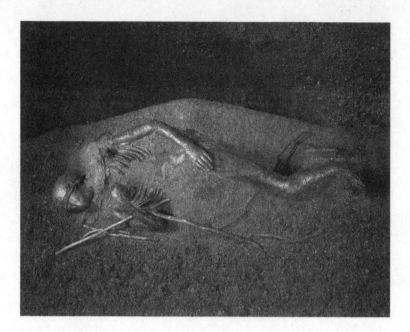

THE WINDEBY CHILD

The Windeby Child was discovered in 1952 by peat cutters in Germany. Bog bodies are well preserved due to the unusual combination of highly acidic water, low temperature, and lack of oxygen that exists in the turf fields.

Research now suggests that the body was that of a sixteen-year-old boy, and that the manner of death was likely natural causes. Lack of trauma is the main evidence for this theory. The half-shaven appearance is thought to be the result of half the scalp being exposed to oxygen longer than the rest of the body, or to damage during discovery.

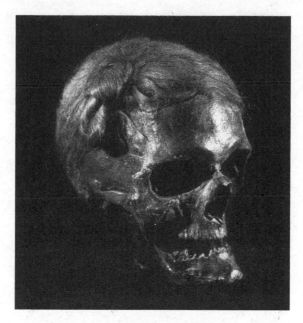

THE OSTERBY MAN

This human head, thought to be from a male decapitated between 70 and 220 AD, was found in the state of Schleswig-Holstein in Germany. He is known as the "Osterby Man" and was found under a peat bog, wrapped in a buckskin cape. His hair is well preserved, unusual for a bog body, and features the distinctive Swabian/Suebian knot frequently tied by men from the Germanic tribe of Suebi. The reddish-brown color is the result of acids from the bog, and it is thought that the hair would have been dark blond and white in life—a potential indication of the man's older age. Although his cause of death is unknown, the decapitation and fractured skull suggest it was a deliberate execution.

EUROPEAN EAGLE-OWL

The European eagle-owl is one of the most widespread species of its kind, inhabiting a range of almost twelve million square miles across Europe and Asia. One of the largest species of owl, it can be identified by its distinctive ear "tufts," with darker colorings, a pattern of dark stripes across the body, and orange eyes. These owls can often be found in rocky or mountainous regions near woodlands, or in wetlands, where they hunt. The European eagle-owl's large size and weight allow them to hunt a wide range of animals. Their primary prey is rodents, but they have also been recorded hunting young rabbits, hedge-hogs, and red foxes. They have one of the longest life spans among owls, living for up to twenty years in the wild.

DISCUSSION QUESTIONS

1. Inspired by the discovery of an ancient bog body in northern Germany, Lois Lowry engaged her powerful curiosity with the mysterious history of the body, only to have the spare facts that archaeologists thought they knew upended by further investigation. How did this unexpected revelation further spark Lowry's imaginative powers?

2. Inherent in the discovery of the Windeby Child is the knowledge that a life has been cut short. What are some ways that the author handled the challenges of telling a story with an established, and troubling, ending?

3. Lowry provides vivid details about the daily tasks and expectations of the villagers. How did the author

balance the historical details of people's lives with creating an engaging story that modern readers can relate to?

4. Lowry's two lead characters have different goals: Estrild is focused on breaking out of the roles expected of her, and Varick is focused on the idea of doing one brave thing. What might have led the author to make these choices for her characters?

5. Memory is a potent theme in several of Lowry's works, including *The Giver* and *On the Horizon*. *The Windeby Puzzle* could be read as an argument for how memory and imagination are defenses against the passage of time. What other qualities or contributions could be thought to withstand the passage of time?

SELECTION OF QUOTES

The below quotes were selected as they capture, in Lowry's potent, direct language, meaningful themes from the book. What does each quote mean to you? Do you agree with the position of the speaker? Are there other quotes that you would call out for further thought?

But she liked the idea of the little skeleton, the remains of a creature taking on a new role, reminding one that it had existed. Usually dead things—even people!—crumbled and rotted away and were forgotten. (p. 25)

Watching them, Estrild had begun to feel a passion to become more than just another wife, one more woman made gaunt from chores and childbearing, old before her time. Women deserved more. (p. 33)

She rehearsed and rehearsed it all in her mind. . . . Estrild smoothed her hair, breathed deeply, and counted to herself the number of nights left until her life, and perhaps the lives of all the girls in her village, including her younger sisters and females yet to be born, would change. (p. 87)

Just a murmur, at first: hushed and tentative. It was a whispered chorus made up of the voices of women and girls. They were asking questions of each other: questions about the future. The soft sound of it cushioned her with hope for them all. (p. 107)

"That it is not time to die until you have done one brave, good thing. My uncle had done that, they told her: had helped his friend on the battlefield. After that, you are ready and people should not be sad because they will always remember you and your one brave, good thing." (pp. 128–29)

About the Author

LOIS LOWRY is known for her versatility and invention as a writer. She is the author of more than forty books. She was born in Hawaii and grew up in New York, Pennsylvania, and Japan. She received Newbery Medals for two of her novels, *Number the Stars* and *The Giver*. She has received countless other honors, among them the *Boston Globe–Horn Book* Award, the Dorothy Canfield Fisher Award, the California Young Reader Medal, and the Mark Twain Award. Ms. Lowry lives in Maine. Visit her at loislowry.com.

More from
LOIS LOWRY